FUN

The manageress came hurrying over.
The check-out assistant handed Peter's
ten-pound note to her. The manageress
held the note up to the light. She turned
to Peter.

'Is this your ten-pound note?'
she asked.

Peter nodded. 'Yes.'

'Do you mind telling me where you
got it?'

'Of course not,' said Peter. 'It was at a
car boot sale. On Saturday. Why, is there
something wrong? Is it stolen?'

'Not stolen, no,' said the manageress,
shaking her head.

'What, then?'

The manageress turned to Peter. She
looked serious.

'I am going to have to call the police,
I'm afraid. This ten-pound note is a fake!'

The Mystery Kids series

THE MYSTERY KIDS
Funny Money

Fiona Kelly

Hodder
Children's
Books

a division of Hodder Headline plc

Special thanks to Michael Coleman

Copyright © 1995 Ben M. Baglio
Created by Ben M. Baglio
London W6 0HE

First published in Great Britain in 1995
by Hodder Children's Books

A Catalogue record for this book is
available from the British Library

ISBN 0 340 61994 5

Typeset by Hewer Text Composition Services, Edinburgh
Printed and bound in Great Britain by
Mackays of Chatham PLC, Chatham, Kent

Hodder Children's Books
a Division of Hodder Headline plc
338 Euston Road
London NW1 3BH

Decisions, decisions

'Do you think I would make a good crook?' asked Holly Adams, trying to look sinister.

'You? A crook?' Holly's best friend, Miranda Hunt, gave a spluttering laugh. 'Never!'

'Why not?' said Holly.

She stood up and looked in the mirror on the wall. Holding her long brown hair out of the way, she tried curling her top lip and snarling at the same time. This only made Miranda let loose one of her louder laughs – which, in Miranda's case, meant very loud.

'Holly, you just haven't got a crook's face. You look much too honest.'

'How about this one, then?' Holly narrowed her eyes, bared her teeth and pressed her nose flat with one finger.

'Now you look like a boxer who's had one fight too many,' laughed Miranda. She shook her head as Holly tried scrunching up one of

1

her ears as well. 'No, if anybody's going to end up as a crook, it's going to be me.'

Miranda levered herself out of her chair and joined Holly in front of the mirror. 'Watch this,' she said.

Taking hold of the end of her long corn-coloured hair, Miranda twisted it into a plait before looping it across her neck and up under her chin. Then she completed the picture by opening her eyes wide and letting her tongue flop out of the corner of her mouth.

'And who are you supposed to be?' said Holly, giggling.

'Not who. What. I'm an evil, wicked murderer.'

'Golly. Do evil, wicked murderers look like that?'

Miranda rolled her eyes and gurgled. 'They do after they've been hanged!'

'Miranda!' squealed Holly. 'You are so *gruesome*!'

'Hey, gruesome. Now that's good.' Miranda flopped back into her chair. 'We could call ourselves the Gruesome Twosome.'

'Oh, wonderful,' laughed Holly. 'I can hear the introduction now.' She held an imaginary microphone in front of her lips. 'And now for the next act in tonight's talent contest. A mystery sketch featuring the one and only Gruesome Twosome!'

'I don't think Mr Taylor would go for that, somehow,' said a muffled voice.

Miranda leaned over and tapped on the side of the tea-chest in the middle of the floor.

'Peter, would you mind repeating that? For some strange reason I've always had trouble understanding people who talk while they've got their head in a box.'

Peter Hamilton extracted himself from the tea-chest, his brown hair flopping over his eyes as he did so. He pushed it away with the back of his hand.

'I was saying, from what I've seen of Mr Taylor I don't think he'd think much of a sketch in the school talent contest starring a couple of girls calling themselves the Gruesome Twosome.'

'I don't see why not,' sniffed Miranda. 'He's pretty gruesome himself, you know. You haven't been going to Thomas Petheridge long enough to find out just how gruesome. Last year he gave me a detention just for laughing!'

Peter grinned. 'Are you sure it was for laughing, Miranda – or for the windows you broke?'

Miranda glared at him; then, seeing Holly giggling, started doing the same herself.

Holly and Miranda had been firm friends for a long time. They shared lots of interests, but especially anything to do with mysteries. They were avid readers of mystery books and watchers of television programmes with a mystery theme. That was why, when she'd heard about the school talent contest, Holly had immediately thought they could act out a mystery sketch.

'OK, OK,' said Miranda when they'd calmed down. 'Forget about the Gruesome Twosome. What are we going to do then?'

'Er . . . excuse me,' said Peter. 'Didn't you say you'd come round to help me sort my things out?'

Miranda forced her face into a frown. 'Did we say that, Holly? I thought we said we'd come round to sort *him* out.'

'You know what we said, Miranda,' laughed Holly.

Miranda grinned. 'Of course I know. That's what friends are for.'

Holly and Miranda had lived in Highgate, in London, for all their twelve years. They'd met Peter after he'd moved to the area with his father, and they'd discovered that he, too, was a mystery fan. They called themselves the Mystery Kids, because they enjoyed investigating any mysterious goings-on they happened to stumble across.

'Get ready for some help then, Peter,' said Miranda. She slipped from her chair and knelt on the floor next to Peter.

Holly went round and knelt down on the other side of him. 'We're looking for things you can sell at tomorrow's car boot sale, right?'

During the Spring term, the grounds of Thomas Petheridge Comprehensive School were used for a car boot sale every Saturday. It had become a very popular event, attracting dozens of cars packed with things their owners wanted to sell, together with hordes of people in search of a bargain. Holly, Miranda and Peter had often picked up a really good mystery book for just a few pence when it would have cost them pounds in a shop.

'Right,' said Peter. 'When Dad said he was

5

planning to sort some things out to take to the sale, I thought it was about time I did the same.'

The Hamiltons had lived in a flat when they'd first moved to Highgate, but now they'd moved to a larger house. This had given them a chance to unpack all the things that they hadn't had room for in the cramped flat.

'The trouble is,' Peter went on, 'I don't seem to have very much to sell.'

'So it seems,' said Holly.

On his bed, Peter had placed two large labels, one reading 'Keep', the other 'Sell'. Every time he'd taken something from the tea-chest he'd placed it behind one of the labels. The 'Keep' pile was very much larger than the 'Sell' pile!

'You see,' said Peter, 'everything I've got I either want to keep, or else I think if I don't keep it I'll want it again one day and I'll wish I'd kept it because then I'll want it.'

Miranda blinked. 'Did you follow that, Holly?'

'Of course,' said Holly. She moved closer. 'Budge up then, Peter. I'm sure Miranda and I can help.'

'Yes, budge up, Peter,' said Miranda, squeezing herself closer on Peter's other side. 'Let's see what you've got in this treasure-chest of yours.'

She stuck an arm into the chest and waggled it around for a moment before pulling out a teddy-bear with one ear missing.

'Here you are. How about this? You could make a few pence on this. If you can *bear* to part with it, of course!'

'Miranda,' groaned Holly, 'your jokes are getting worse.'

'Not possible,' smiled Peter. He reached out and took the bear from Miranda. 'Anyway, Tarzan's not for sale.'

'Tarzan!' screeched Miranda. 'His name's *Tarzan*!'

'You used to call your teddy Grin-Grin,' said Holly. 'What sort of name is that?'

'A good name,' said Miranda. 'But *Tarzan*!'

Peter placed the bear carefully in the 'Keep' pile. 'Now are you two going to help me or not? I'm trying to get ready for tomorrow's car boot sale, you know, not next week's.'

'How about this?' said Holly, yanking a worn old cricket bat from the tea-chest.

'That can go,' said Peter, pleased at last to

find something he definitely didn't want. He tossed it on to the 'Sell' pile.

Miranda looked at the bat thoughtfully. 'How much do you want for it? I might buy it.'

Holly looked at her best friend. 'A cricket bat?' she said. 'Since when have you played cricket, Miranda?'

'I don't want it for playing cricket,' said Miranda. 'I thought it might come in handy for our mystery sketch.'

'How?'

'We could do the bit out of *Oliver Twist*,' said Miranda, picking the bat up and holding it above her head. 'You know, where rotten old Bill Sykes goes after poor little Nancy and beats her brains out . . .'

'Miranda, no!' squealed Holly.

'Aren't we going to need a blunt instrument, then? All decent mysteries have a blunt instrument in them somewhere.'

'Miranda, I really don't think we want to do that sort of sketch.'

'What sort of sketch *do* we want to do?'

'Not that sort. Something a bit more . . . subtle,' said Holly.

'Like what?'

'Like . . .' Holly snapped her fingers. 'A scene out of *Spyglass*? How about that?'

Spyglass was the one television programme they all watched without fail. They liked to compare notes after every episode, saying how they thought the hero – Secret Agent John Raven – was going to get out of the sticky situation he'd found himself in.

Holly turned up the collar of her blouse and leaned nonchalantly against Peter's wardrobe door. 'I could be John Raven,' she said.

Miranda shook her head in short sharp jerks, her hair flicking from side to side. 'Nooo, Holly. I don't think so. You haven't got the John Raven look. He's more cool and languid than that.'

'Languid. What's languid?'

'Loose and casual,' said Miranda, standing up. 'Like this.'

She let her arms flop to her sides, then slouched across the room before falling into Peter's chair in a fit of the giggles.

'In case it's escaped your notice,' said Peter, 'John Raven is a man. Perhaps I should join this sketch?'

'No, thanks,' said Miranda at once.

Holly shook her head. 'Sorry, Peter.'

'It's not that we don't think you're talented and handsome and – what else, Holly?'

'Brilliant and witty,' said Holly, 'but . . .'

'A first prize shared between two is bigger than a first prize shared between three,' interrupted Peter with a laugh. 'Don't worry, I wasn't serious.'

He looked at his watch. 'Now, do you think we can get on with this? The sale starts at nine o'clock and I was thinking I might like to go to bed between now and then.'

Miranda and Holly dropped to the floor beside him again. Holly pulled a board from the tea-chest. It was covered with a jumble of wires and small electrical components.

'How about this?' she said. 'Somebody might want it – if they can work out what it is.'

'It's a crystal set. A primitive radio. It was the first thing I ever remember making with my dad. When I say "made", my dad made it, and I sort of held things. I can still remember Mum's face when she heard a music programme coming out of it. She couldn't believe it.'

For a moment, Peter looked thoughtful and sad at the same time. Holly and Miranda both knew why. Peter's mother had died when he was quite young. Holly carefully put the old crystal set on to the 'Keep' pile.

'How about this, Peter? This *must* go!'

Miranda had pulled a bright orange box from the tea-chest. It had clearly been well used. The lid was stained and needed two large elastic bands to hold it on. Slipping the elastic bands off, Miranda looked inside.

'Ugh!'

'Hey, my old chemistry set!' cried Peter.

He pulled the box towards him. Inside, each in its own specially shaped foam-rubber compartment, were rows of small bottles and test-tubes. Some had different coloured liquids and powders inside. Peter lifted one out.

'Iron-filings,' he said. 'Do you know what you can do with something as simple as iron-filings?'

'No,' said Holly.

'Spell it properly?' said Miranda, pointing at the test-tube. Its handwritten label had been misspelt so that it read 'iron-fillings'.

'My spelling's not as good as my chemistry,' grinned Peter. He continued ferreting in the box. 'There's nothing missing. Look.

Even the bunsen burner's still here.' He lifted it out thoughtfully. 'I wonder if it works? I could try it out . . .'

'Now who's wasting time?' said Miranda.

'I think we all are,' said Holly. 'Come on, Miranda. I think we've given Peter as much help as he can use for one day.'

As Holly headed for the door, Miranda got to her feet. 'Hang on, Holly.' She turned to Peter. 'I've just had a brilliant idea. This will solve all your problems, Peter.'

'Oh, yes?'

'Definitely,' said Miranda. 'Watch.'

Stepping across the floor to Peter's bed, she picked up the 'Keep' label in one hand and the 'Sell' label in the other.

Then, twirling them in the air, she spun round a couple of times – and slapped the labels down against opposite piles. 'There you go!'

'Thanks, Miranda,' grinned Peter. 'I don't know how I'd manage without you both.'

Holly laughed. 'Peter, you say the nicest things!'

'Doesn't he just?' said Miranda. 'But he's right. I don't know how he'd manage without us either.' She looked at Peter and grinned.

'So . . . why don't we come along tomorrow and help you out?'

Peter held his hands in the air. 'No, it's all right. I can manage on my own.'

Holly and Miranda looked at each other. 'Mystery Kids,' said Holly.

'A team,' said Miranda.

'It's our duty, Miranda.'

'It is, Holly.'

They laughed. 'See you tomorrow, Peter!' Holly called as she clicked open the front door and they ran out.

 **Disguises**

Mr Hamilton's car looked as though it was about to burst.

'I take it all back, Peter,' said Miranda as they met the car at the school gates. 'You do know how to get rid of things.'

'Is *all* this stuff yours?' asked Holly, pointing at the pile of boxes and cartons in the back.

Peter leaned out of the passenger window. 'Er . . . not all of it.'

Mr Hamilton leaned across from the driving seat. 'You see that box at the back? Behind the lampshade?'

'The little one?' said Miranda.

'Yes. That's Peter's. The rest of the stuff is mine. I don't think he'd have brought anything at all if it hadn't been for you two,' said Mr Hamilton. 'So, well done.'

As the man at the gate came across,

15

Mr Hamilton pulled some coins from his pocket and paid his entrance fee.

'They're with us,' he said, when the man asked about Holly and Miranda. 'We just didn't have enough room to fit them in.'

Putting the car into gear, Mr Hamilton moved through the school gates and on into the school grounds. A number of cars were already in position. Most had their boot lids up, their owners busy unloading what they'd brought to sell. A lot of them had set up long portable decorating tables, and were laying out their goods as if they were running a stall in the market.

Mr Hamilton had brought his own table. After he'd been ushered into a vacant parking spot, it was the first thing that he unloaded from the back of the car.

'Why don't you take that end, Peter,' he said when the table was up, 'and I'll have this end. We can fight over the space in the middle.'

'No contest,' said Holly, as the unloading got under way.

Unlike Peter, Mr Hamilton seemed to have had no trouble deciding what to get rid of. Soon his end, the middle, and part of

Peter's end of the table were laid out with lampshades, old tools, a stack of books, cassette tapes and countless other small items. Other things, including a golf bag, a push-along lawn-mower, and an engraving kit in a smart grey case, he'd spread out on a plastic sheet on the ground in front of him.

'Sherlock Holmes?' said Holly, unable to resist a quick look at the books Mr Hamilton had brought.

'*The Complete Sherlock Holmes Long Stories*,' said Mr Hamilton. 'Five hundred and seventy-one pages of mystery for just . . . what? Twenty-five pence?'

'I'll take it,' said Holly. 'I can review it for *The Tom-tom*.'

The Tom-tom was the name of the lower-school magazine that she and Miranda produced. Holly wrote a mystery column for it, describing any good mystery books or television programmes they'd seen. Miranda's speciality was the bad jokes column.

'I thought you were here to help me,' said Peter, 'not buy up the competition's merchandise.'

Holly tucked the book away. All around them, people were bustling about.

17

'What time do they let in the hordes?' asked Miranda.

'Ten o'clock,' said Peter, hurriedly arranging his own end of the table. 'Not long now. Get ready for the rush.'

All around there seemed to be items of just about every description available for sale.

'How about a mystery sketch set in a car boot sale?' Miranda said. 'One of us could play a suspicious stall-holder.'

'Selling stolen goods, you mean?' said Holly. 'Could be.'

She looked around. Nearby, an old man had set up a stall with nothing on it but clocks.

'Like him,' said Holly. 'Now there's an idea. You could be a spy, with clocks that have got stolen information stuffed inside – or maybe they've got microdots between the minutes on the clock face.'

Miranda bent almost double and croaked, 'Roll up, roll up. Get your secrets here.'

'And I could play John Raven,' said Holly. 'I'll uncover what you're doing and have you arrested.'

Miranda straightened up. 'Possibly, possibly. You could say to me, "False clocks, eh? You'll do time for this"!'

18

Holly shook her head in despair. 'Miranda, you get worse.'

Peter had finished laying out the contents of his box. 'I see Tarzan stayed at home,' said Miranda.

'Miranda,' said Peter, 'if you'd had your way I'd have sold everything I own!'

'He *has* brought his old chemistry set, Miranda,' said Holly. She pointed to the bright orange box Peter had placed in a prominent position at the front of the table. 'It's still in good condition, Peter. I'm sure somebody will buy it.'

'I think my dad's hoping so,' said Peter. 'He reminded me last night I scorched a cupboard the last time I used it.'

'Well, you must stand a chance of selling it. There's enough people here,' said Miranda.

Outside the school gates a long queue of buyers had formed. At ten o'clock on the dot the gates opened and in they all rushed, spreading quickly amongst the different cars and stalls, picking things up, examining them, paying for them. The Hamiltons' car was quite far from the gate, but a small crowd very soon gathered round them.

'How much for the book-ends?' an elegant

lady asked Mr Hamilton. Beside her, as though he thought he might be in for a long wait, a grey-haired man settled himself on to a shooting-stick.

Peter's father picked up the pair of heavy wooden book-ends. 'Two pounds?' he suggested.

The woman looked doubtful. Turning, she said to the man, 'What do you think, Horace?'

He shrugged. 'Don't look at me, Ethel.'

'Not a lot of help, my husband,' said the woman. She looked again at the book-ends, as if unable to make up her mind.

'Tell you what,' said Mr Hamilton, 'I'll throw in the lampshade for nothing. How's that?'

The woman thought for a moment, then nodded. 'Done,' she said. She turned once again to the man and held her hand out. Holly and Miranda watched as he dipped into his inside pocket and pulled out a ten-pound note. Mr Hamilton counted out the change and the couple went off.

'Your dad's made a good start,' Holly said to Peter.

'I'm glad somebody has,' said Peter as a

group of people passed by his end of the table without a second glance.

'You need to drum up business,' said Miranda. 'Let them know you're here. Like they do at the market.'

'What – *shout*, you mean?'

'Of course,' said Miranda. She leaned over the front of the table. 'Come along, now. Look at our great offers! Happy Hamilton's is the place! Every one a bargain.'

A teenager wearing a windcheater with a tiger embroidered on the back stopped to look at some computer games Peter didn't play any more.

'How much?' he asked.

'Three pounds each?' said Peter.

As the teenager thought things over, Miranda leaned across the table and tapped her finger on the orange box.

'See this chemistry set? Look, it's got everything. Even iron-filings. Buy two of those computer games and he'll throw in this chemistry set for nothing. Can't say fairer than that now, can he?'

'Done!' said the teenager immediately.

Peter clamped his hand down on the chemistry set. 'No, I won't!' he said.

'I thought you wanted to get rid of this stuff?' said Miranda as the teenager drifted away empty-handed.

'For money,' said Peter. 'I don't want to give it away!'

Holly looped her arm through Miranda's and tugged gently. 'Shall we go for a look round?' she said. 'There might be some good books on some of the stalls.'

'I don't know, Holly,' said Miranda. 'Peter needs me.'

'I'm prepared to struggle on alone, Miranda,' Peter said with a grin. 'But don't worry; if I do decide to give everything away then I'll definitely give you a call.'

Holly and Miranda wandered off. If anything, the crowds were even thicker now as people continued to come in through the main gate.

The two girls meandered past stalls selling everything from plants to paintings before Holly spotted one which had a large collection of books laid out on a table.

Soon Holly was totally engrossed as she scanned the titles, looking for any mystery books she hadn't read – or for another copy of *Harriet the Spy*, her all-time favourite book.

Three copies, if possible. It was Miranda and Peter's favourite book too, and their copies, just like her own, were falling apart through over-use.

'See anything interesting, Miranda?' said Holly as she finally reached the end of the long line of books. But her friend was no longer at her side.

Holly turned away from the stall and pushed her way out through the jostle of people around her. It really was a popular boot sale. The school grounds were thronged with people now, the most there'd been all morning.

Where was Miranda? Holly looked at her watch and realised she'd lost track of the time. She'd spent ages looking at the books. Perhaps Miranda had wandered back to help Peter again? If that was the case, Holly thought, she'd better join them quickly! She headed back towards Mr Hamilton's car.

But as Holly arrived back at the Hamiltons' stall she saw no sign of Miranda. Or of Peter, for that matter. Only Mr Hamilton, talking to a man who was looking intently at the engraving set in its grey case.

'Will you take ten pounds?' Holly heard the man say as she drew closer.

Mr Hamilton looked doubtful. 'Fifteen?'

'How about twelve?'

Peter's father thought for a moment, then nodded. Holly studied the man as he took out his money, imagining herself to be John Raven on a spying mission and the man a major suspect. He was smartly dressed, she noticed. His sports jacket looked new. So did his brown trousers with their razor-sharp creases. But his shoes were so scuffed and marked they looked as though they'd been bought a thousand years ago.

She watched as the man took out two crisp ten-pound notes and handed them to Mr Hamilton. Then Peter's father counted out a five-pound note and three one-pound coins in change. It was just then that Peter called out from the car.

'There you are! I was just about ready to report you two missing.'

Peter climbed out from the passenger seat. In his hand was the little tin he'd brought with him to hold his takings.

'How have you been doing?' asked Holly.

'Not too bad,' said Peter. He looked quite pleased. Holly noticed now that his end of the shared table was looking a lot clearer.

The old chemistry set was still there, but Peter had obviously sold quite a few things while they'd been away.

'Have you made much money?' she asked.

'Over ten pounds,' said Peter. 'More than I'd have made if Miranda had been here, I think!' He looked around. 'Where is she, anyway?'

Holly looked at him. 'You haven't seen her, then?'

Peter shook his head. 'No. She hasn't been back here.'

'Then I've lost her,' said Holly. She laughed as Peter's face creased into a wide smile. 'And don't look so pleased. I know you don't mean it!'

As the crowds dwindled, Mr Hamilton ducked into the front of his car and pulled out a newspaper that he'd tucked inside the windscreen. He opened it at the cross-word page.

'I think that's the early rush finished,' he said. 'Another half-hour and we might as well get moving, Peter. I've a lot to do today, and I've sold most of my things.'

'OK,' said Peter. 'Maybe Miranda will turn up by then.'

Mr Hamilton dug a hand into his jacket pocket and pulled out a collection of coins. 'Fancy a hot-dog?' he said.

Holly and Peter didn't need asking twice. 'Get one for me, too, will you?' said Mr Hamilton, handing over some money.

'And one for Miranda?' asked Peter. 'The smell might bring her back.'

'Of course,' said Mr Hamilton. 'Go on, I can look after both ends of the table until you get back.'

Peter and Holly wandered off towards the main gates. A small mobile kiosk was selling refreshments there, a plume of steam rising from a little chimney in its roof.

The queue at the refreshments kiosk was quite long, so it took a while before they reached the front.

'Four hot-dogs please,' ordered Peter.

'Extra tomato sauce for Miranda,' said Holly. 'She always likes to do her Dracula impersonation.'

'I suppose we will see her again,' Peter said as they left the kiosk and headed back.

'Hollyyy!' Miranda's loud voice cut through the air like a laser beam.

'I think we're about to,' said Holly. They

turned – and stopped, barely able to suppress their laughter. Behind them, perched on a suitcase, was Miranda, waving her arms.

'It is Miranda, isn't it?' said Peter, chuckling.

Holly tried to keep a straight face. 'It certainly looks like her.'

'Long fair hair. Jeans. Sweater . . .'

'Bowler hat,' said Holly, starting to giggle.

'Sunglasses,' said Peter, laughing.

'False nose, moustache, cigarette holder . . .'

'Yes, it's Miranda all right,' said Peter. 'Hello, Miranda.'

As they walked towards her, Miranda took the cigarette holder from between her teeth and whipped off the mask she was wearing.

'Well, what do you think?' she cried. 'Aren't they brilliant?'

'Ye-es,' Holly said slowly.

'I got them over there.' Miranda pointed to the far corner of the school grounds.

In the distance a tall man, wearing a long-sleeved shirt and what looked like a shoe-lace tie, was opening the rear doors of a rather rusty blue van.

'What, from him?' said Holly, as the man

tossed an orange box into the back of the van and slammed the doors shut.

'No, not him,' said Miranda. 'He wasn't selling anything. From the woman whose car was next to him. It looks like she's gone now, but she was telling me all about how she used to be the secretary of an amateur dramatic society, and about all the shows they put on, and how she'd given it all up now and had turned out her attic and brought all her stuff here and . . .'

'Slow down, Miranda!' said Holly.

Miranda took a deep breath. 'Anyway, it took me ages to get her to agree, but I did in the end. She let me take everything I wanted.'

'You mean – there's more?' said Peter.

'Loads of it,' said Miranda. 'In here.'

She stood up and clicked open the lid of the old suitcase she'd been sitting on. 'Look at it all!' she said.

The case was packed. Hats jostled with scarfs, spectacles with handbags, gloves with more peculiar masks. 'There's even a trench coat in there that would fit John Raven!'

'Well, what do you think?' said Miranda,

pulling out a handbag and strutting up and down with it over her arm. 'Two pounds for the lot.'

'Two pounds?' said Peter.

'Yup. Two pounds. Good, eh?'

Peter shook his head slowly. 'I think she should have given you more than that, Miranda,' he said.

'What?' said Miranda, looking baffled.

Holly joined in. 'Peter's right. Fancy only giving you two pounds to take all her stuff away.'

'She didn't pay *me*. I paid her!'

Miranda's face broke into a grin. She swung the handbag at Holly. 'All right. But I'll have you know, Holly Adams, that this lot is just what we need!'

'It is?'

'Of course it is! Call yourself an actress? What have I got here if it isn't all the props we're likely to need for our mystery sketch? And you never know when these disguises might come in useful. We could be undercover spies!'

Holly wasn't too sure about that, but Miranda was so enthusiastic she didn't have the heart to say so. Instead, she helped her

29

carry the suitcase back to Mr Hamilton's car. By then, Peter's father had started packing things away.

'I thought we were going to leave with less than we'd brought,' he said, eyeing Miranda's suitcase, 'but it looks like I was wrong.'

'Oh, thanks, Mr Hamilton,' beamed Miranda. 'I knew you'd offer to give it a lift home.'

'Did you sell any more while we were away, Dad?' asked Peter.

'A few things,' said Mr Hamilton, biting hungrily into his hot-dog. 'Enough to make room for our travelling salesperson here.'

'None of this lot's for sale,' said Miranda. 'This is now the property of the Mystery Kids!'

As Holly and Miranda helped Mr Hamilton load the suitcase into the car, Peter emptied out his takings. He began sifting through his pile of coins.

'Would you like me to take that loose change off you, Peter?' said Mr Hamilton. 'I can use it in the vending machine at work.'

'OK,' said Peter, who'd been wondering

what he was going to do with all the coins he'd accumulated.

Mr Hamilton dug into his jacket pocket. But as he pulled out one ten-pound note, the others he'd taken that morning came with it and fluttered to the ground. Holly dived across and picked them up before they blew away.

'Thanks, Holly!' said Mr Hamilton as Holly gave them back to him. He then handed one of the notes to Peter, who gave him a pile of coins in return.

'You did pretty well,' said Holly as Peter totalled up his takings.

'Better than I thought,' said Peter.

Mr Hamilton looked up from his final job of folding up their portable table. 'Ah. That's because I sold your old chemistry set while you were away getting the hot-dogs. Good, eh?'

'Great,' said Peter.

But Holly didn't think he looked as though he really meant it.

3 A fake!

'I've got it!' yelled Holly.

'Got what?' asked Miranda. She sat down next to her friend.

'What we can do for our mystery sketch. It came to me in the middle of History this afternoon.'

It was Monday, and school had just finished for the day. The two girls were in the school grounds, sitting on a bench while they waited for Peter to come out.

'Come on then,' said Miranda. 'What's the great idea?'

'A Sherlock Holmes sketch!' Holly said excitedly. 'I've been reading that book I bought from Mr Hamilton at the boot sale on Saturday. In one of the stories, Sherlock Holmes tells Dr Watson about his brother's life story just by looking at his watch!'

'So . . .' said Miranda, 'your idea is that we

do a sketch where good old Sherlock does a bit of deduction from the clues he finds on some object?'

'Yes!'

Miranda let the idea sink in. 'Not bad,' she said. 'Not bad at all. What object can we use? Hey – Peter's cricket bat!'

'He sold it.'

Miranda tutted. 'There you are. I told you our sketch would need a blunt instrument.'

'No, it won't. I was thinking of something a bit different. What if we picked somebody from the audience and got them to turn out their pockets . . .'

'Ye-es,' said Miranda uncertainly. 'Assume I've picked on Mr Taylor. Go on. What happens next?'

'Next we do what Sherlock Holmes would do,' said Holly. 'Try to make some deductions from what they've got on them.'

'I get the idea,' said Miranda. 'How about a bit of practice now?' She peered over towards the double doors which led into the school science block. 'I deduce from the appearance of that boy just coming out that his name is Peter Hamilton and that he is late. Why, Holmes?'

'Elementary, my dear Watson,' said Holly as Peter headed their way, his bag over his shoulder. 'His timetable is different from ours. Today is Monday, and on Monday his last lesson is a double period of science. He's probably been completing some experiment and lost track of the time.'

'An experiment?' Miranda went goggle-eyed. 'Look at his hair, Holmes.'

As usual, Peter's hair was flopping down over his eyes.

'You don't think he's been trying the same experiment that our good friend Dr Jekyll tried . . .'

Holly and Miranda were still laughing when Peter reached them. Holly told him about their Sherlock Holmes idea as they headed out of school.

'Right,' Peter said simply.

'Is that all you've got to say?' said Miranda. 'Don't you think it's a brilliant idea?'

'Yes.'

'What – "yes", you think it's a brilliant idea, or "yes", that's all you've got to say?' asked Holly.

'Both.'

They walked on in silence for a moment.

Then Miranda let out a little yelp. 'Hey! I've just had another idea!'

'What?' said Holly.

'The things I bought at the car boot sale on Saturday,' bubbled Miranda. 'We can use them. They're perfect. I could play Dr Watson, and wear the false nose and moustache. You could be Sherlock Holmes, Holly, and wear the sunglasses.'

'Sherlock Holmes didn't wear sunglasses,' muttered Peter. 'He used a magnifying glass.'

'And the bowler hat,' Miranda went on, 'Sherlock could wear the bowler hat. And use the cigarette holder.'

Peter shook his head. 'Sherlock Holmes wore a deerstalker hat, not a bowler hat. And he sucked a pipe. He was famous for it.'

Miranda exploded. 'Well this is going to be a sketch about Sherlock Holmes *before* he became famous!' she yelled. 'Peter, what is the matter with you?'

'Nothing,' said Peter.

Holly looked at their friend. He certainly seemed to have had something on his mind since he came out of school.

'Are you sure?' she said.

Peter stopped and sighed. 'Well, yes. There is something. We've just had double Science.'

'Oh, well,' said Miranda, 'you're forgiven. Two whole periods of Science is enough to make anybody miserable.'

'I thought you liked Science,' said Holly.

'That's the whole point,' said Peter, 'I do. We spent the whole time doing a chemistry experiment. It was really good. Now I'm wishing I hadn't sold my old chemistry set. I really fancy doing some experiments again.'

'Science? Out of school?' Miranda put a finger to the side of her head and waggled it back and forth. 'Is this boy loopy?'

Together they walked out of the school gates. Turning left, they walked slowly along to the end of the block. Then, they turned again and walked along the side of the school.

'Can't you buy another chemistry set out of the money you made?' asked Holly.

'Not really,' said Peter. 'They're very expensive. I haven't got enough.' He sighed. 'I'm just going to have to put that money in the bank and save up until I've got enough for a new one. Pity . . .'

'Why?'

'Because what we did in Science today has given me an idea for a really *brilliant* experiment.'

Holly turned to him. 'I bet it has, knowing you!'

Peter smiled. 'Look, I'm sorry if I didn't seem to think much of your idea. I do. A Sherlock Holmes and Dr Watson sketch will be great.'

'Even with Sherlock in a bowler hat?' said Miranda.

'Of course,' said Peter. 'Didn't you know that he was also a master of disguise?'

'He was?'

'Definitely. You could have him wear everything in your suitcase, Miranda.'

'A master of disguise,' said Miranda. 'Hey, we could have Dr Watson telling the audience, "Dis guy's in disguise"!'

Peter and Holly groaned at the awful joke. Cheerful again, and chattering happily, they walked along the road.

Some distance along, at the point where the main school buildings ended, was a small side entrance which led in behind the kitchens. A row of oblong wheelie-bins was lined up behind the railings. As they drew near they saw Powell, the school caretaker, dragging a large black sack towards one of the bins.

'Holmes,' whispered Miranda to Holly. 'That man! Is he a robber, getting away with the school dinner money?'

'No, Watson,' Holly whispered back. 'Look at his sack. It doesn't have "Swag" on the side.'

'Then who can he be?' said Miranda. 'Surely not . . . Father Christmas?'

'Wrong time of the year, Watson.'

Miranda rubbed her chin. 'This could be his summer job.'

They drew level with the bins just as Powell reached them.

'Car boot sales,' the caretaker grumbled aloud. 'Nothing but trouble. Don't know how much money they make for the school, but I know how much extra work they make for me – and it's a lot.'

Still muttering, he tossed back the lid of the nearest bin. It was almost full to the brim. 'I shouldn't have to do this,' Powell moaned. 'In the good old days, the refuse collectors came in to get all this for themselves.'

'Now they just refuse, eh?' joked Miranda.

Powell looked blank.

'Joke?' said Miranda.

'I don't think he got it, Miranda,' said Peter as they walked on.

He turned to look back at the caretaker. Powell was standing on tiptoe, heaving the contents of the bin to one side to make some room for the sack he'd brought out. As he did so, a box fell out.

Peter stopped dead.

As he stood there, Powell heaved his black sack up into the bin. Then, tossing the box back on top of everything else, he jammed down the wheelie-bin lid as far as it would go and shuffled off back into the school.

'So what is this experiment you want to try, Peter?' Holly asked as she and Miranda reached the end of the road. 'Peter?'

Realising that Peter was no longer with them, Holly and Miranda turned round. As they watched, he ran in through the side gate and over to the wheelie-bin that Powell had just been using.

'What are you doing?' Holly called as Peter started to lift the wheelie-bin's lid.

'Maybe he's going off collecting car numbers,' said Miranda, referring to one of Peter's favourite hobbies. 'Maybe he's starting a black sack collection instead.'

Holly had to admit that it did look a bit like it. Holding the lid up with one hand, Peter certainly seemed to be looking intently into the bin.

'Help!' he shouted suddenly.

Holly and Miranda ran back. 'What is it?'

'Quick. Can you hold this lid up for me?'

'Why?'

'Because, I thought I saw . . .' With both hands free, Peter dug both hands into the bin – and pulled out the box that Powell the caretaker had thrown back in moments before. A battered orange box that they'd all seen before. 'I did! Look. It's my old chemistry set!'

'Yours?' said Holly. 'Peter, it can't be yours. Your dad sold it on Saturday.'

'It *is* mine. Look.'

Through the badly ripped lid, Holly saw the proof even before Peter pointed to it.

'The iron filings,' she said.

Peter lifted out the test-tube Holly was talking about. 'See. It's my misspelt label.' The label read: 'iron fillings'.

41

'You're right,' said Miranda. 'It *is* your old chemistry set.'

'The bunsen burner's missing,' said Peter. A shaped pocket in the foam rubber was empty. 'Apart from that, though, it's all here.'

Holly looked thoughtful. This was a mystery. 'Why would somebody buy something and then throw it away?'

'Because they realised they'd bought a load of old rubbish?' said Miranda.

She held up her hands as Peter gave her a sharp look. 'Only joking, Peter. Anyway, even if somebody had thought that, they'd have returned it to your dad and asked for their money back.'

'I wonder who *did* buy it?' said Peter.

'Who knows?' said Miranda. 'Anyway, Peter. It looks like it's your lucky day.'

'Double lucky day,' said Holly. 'You've got your chemistry set back *and* you've got the money.'

Miranda hooted. 'You can sell it again next week!'

Peter laughed. 'I don't know about that. I think I might hang on to it this time.' He dipped a hand into his pocket and pulled out his ten-pound note.

'But you're right, Holly, I *have* got the money as well. Come on. Let's call in at the supermarket on the way home. The doughnuts are on me!'

When they arrived at the supermarket, Miranda pulled a trolley out from the line outside the swish glass doors and half-pushed, half-scooted it towards the entrance.

Unfortunately the trolley wasn't as smooth-running as the glass doors. It wobbled from side to side.

'Help!' said Miranda as the trolley veered off to one side. 'This thing's alive! What is it about trolleys!'

Before they'd got together as the Mystery Kids, Holly and Miranda had once spied on Peter in this very shop – an episode which had ended with all three of them being thrown out after an unfortunate collision between Miranda's trolley and a tower of baked-bean cans!

Holly dashed forward and took hold of the trolley's front. Together they steered it safely away from the queue of people waiting to use the cash machine set into the wall beside the supermarket's front doors.

As they struggled past, the woman at the head of the queue let out a cry of irritation.

Holly noticed that the message that had just flashed up on the cash machine's small green screen said: 'UNABLE TO DISPENSE CASH'.

'It's run out!' the woman said to the man behind her.

The woman took her cash card as it popped out and was about to return it to her purse when the man behind said, 'It's all right. We're in luck. Here comes the money, by the look of it.'

A dark-green security van, its small rear windows covered with grilles, had just drawn up on the forecourt outside the supermarket's doors. The driver, in a matching dark green uniform, climbed out and threw open the rear doors. He slid out two oblong metal boxes, one in each hand.

'Come on, dear, we're all here waiting for you,' cried the woman at the head of the queue for the cash machine. She pulled out the pockets of her coat to show that they were empty. 'See!'

The security guard was wearing a large helmet, with a visor which came down so low that all Holly could tell about the man's face was that he had a beard. 'All right, all right,' the security guard growled. 'I'm going as fast as I can.'

The doors swished open as Peter, Holly and Miranda went through. They heard the clank of the boxes as the security guard followed them.

Holly and Miranda were still trying to control the trolley. As the guard tried to push past them, the trolley swung in front of him.

'Come on you kids, out of the way,' he snapped.

'All right, all right, we're going as fast as we can,' said Miranda loudly.

With a big effort she heaved the shopping trolley over to one side. The security guard flipped up the visor of his helmet as he shoved by. 'And about time too,' he said sourly.

He stopped, almost at once, outside a door marked 'Private'. A woman in a crisp blouse and black skirt was waiting there. The supermarket's manageress, assumed Holly, noticing that she had a bunch of keys attached to her waistband.

The manageress selected one of the keys and opened the door. She went in, followed by the guard who swept into the room without bothering to close the door behind him.

'That must be the other side of the cash machine,' said Peter, stopping to peer through the open door. Holly and Miranda stopped beside him to watch what was happening.

The manageress selected another key from the bunch at her waist, then inserted it into the lock of what looked like a large safe set into the wall of the room. The security guard put a key from his own bunch into a second lock in the safe door. They turned their keys at the same time. Finally, the guard grabbed hold of the large handle in the centre of the door and swung it open. Inside it seemed to be full of machinery.

'That's where the money goes, is it?' said Holly. 'The bit with the boxes in?'

The guard was pulling a box out of a rack in the centre of the machine's works.

'They're called hoppers,' said Peter. 'They have one for five- and twenty-pound notes, and usually two hoppers of ten-pound notes.'

He watched carefully as the guard put one

he said mysteriously, 'but they're not for eating.'

'Peter,' said Holly. 'What are you up to?'

'Chemistry,' said Peter, smiling.

Holly didn't press him. Peter's habit of keeping little plans to himself could be infuriating, but she knew that they were also entertaining. She could wait.

'Why don't you two get the doughnuts?' he said.

'Because we want to see what you're up to,' said Miranda. 'We can get the doughnuts on the way.'

'OK,' grinned Peter.

He led them first to the greengrocery section. Then to the beverages section. Finally, via the bakery section where they bought their doughnuts, they ended up in the pickles and spices section.

'We could use a supermarket setting for our mystery sketch, Holly,' said Miranda as they joined the end of a check-out queue.

She pretended to peer through a magnifying glass at the things Peter had collected in the shopping basket.

'Half a red cabbage, an onion, a lemon, a packet of tea, and a small bottle of vinegar.

48

What do you make of this little lot, Holmes? Suspicious, eh?'

Holly joined in the fun. 'Watson, I would say that this boy has been collecting all the ingredients necessary for the manufacture of gunpowder.'

Miranda looked aghast. 'You don't mean – you suspect him of plotting to blow up Thomas Petheridge Comprehensive School?'

'Definitely. Mark my words, Watson. I'm willing to bet that this villain has traces of vinegar on his school sweater, and fragments of red cabbage in his trouser turn-ups!'

The check-out queue moved forward. Peter placed his basket on the end shelf and unloaded the things he'd bought. The check-out assistant swiped them one by one across the magic eye.

'Three pounds, twenty-four pence, please.'

Peter handed over his ten-pound note. The check-out assistant held the note up to the light for a moment. She glanced at Peter, then held the note up to the light again. Finally she leaned forward and rang the bell at the side of the till.

'Maybe it's stolen,' Miranda whispered to Holly. She peered at the note through her pretend magnifying glass. 'What do you make of this, Holmes?'

Holly didn't answer. Could it be stolen? She knew that all bank-notes had their own unique serial number. Had the assistant checked it against a list of stolen notes without them seeing?

As the bell rang again, the manageress came hurrying over. The check-out assistant handed Peter's ten-pound note to her, whispering something that Holly couldn't catch.

This time the manageress held the note up to the light. She turned to Peter.

'Is this your ten-pound note?' she asked.

Peter nodded. 'Yes.'

'Do you mind telling me where you got it?'

'Of course not,' said Peter. 'It was at a car boot sale. On Saturday.'

The manageress looked serious. 'I don't suppose you could describe the person who gave it to you.'

Peter smiled. 'I think I probably could. It was my father.'

'Your father?'

'Yes. Why, is there something wrong? Is that money stolen?'

'Not stolen, no,' said the manageress, shaking her head.

'What, then?'

The manageress turned to Peter. She looked serious.

'I am going to have to call the police, I'm afraid. This ten-pound note is a fake.'

4 Suspects

'So, Mr Hamilton, you do confirm that you gave your son this ten-pound note?' asked the police officer.

Peter's father, still out of breath after the hurried dash from the architect's office where he worked, looked again at the bank-note the officer was holding.

'Well . . . yes,' he said. 'I certainly gave Peter a ten-pound note, in return for a pile of loose change. If that's the one he had with him, than I assume that's it.' Mr Hamilton gave a nervous shrug of the shoulders. 'I mean, they all look pretty much the same, don't they?'

The police officer jotted something in his notebook before answering.

'You're right, sir. This note does look pretty much the same as any other. That's the problem. It's a very good forgery indeed.'

'The check-out girl spotted it though, didn't she?' said Holly.

'That's girls for you,' said Miranda. 'You can rely on us.'

The manageress gave a little laugh. 'That may be one reason,' she said. 'But a more likely one is that all our staff are trained to spot counterfeit notes. She knew what she was looking for.'

'What *was* she looking for?' asked Holly eagerly. This was interesting. Already she'd started thinking of this whole episode as a potential article for the mystery column in *The Tom-tom*.

'A silver thread, for one thing,' said the manageress. She held up a genuine ten-pound note for them to see, pointing at the line of silver dashes which ran through the word 'TEN'.

'But . . . didn't that counterfeit note have a silver thread too?' said Peter.

'Yes. But there's a difference.' This time the manageress held the note up to the light. 'You see? On the surface, the thread looks as though it's a line of dashes. But when you hold it up to the light you see . . .'

'A *solid* line!' exclaimed Holly, gazing up at the genuine ten-pound note.

'Now look at the silver line on this one,' said the manageress. She took the counterfeit note from the police officer and held it up to the light.

'It doesn't become solid,' said Peter. 'It stays as a line of dashes.'

'Why?' asked Miranda.

The police officer answered. 'Because the silver thread goes *through* a genuine banknote. With that forgery, the silver's been printed on top.'

'There is another check,' said the manageress. She held the good note up to the light again. 'You see the picture of the Queen?'

'It's a watermark, isn't it?' said Peter. 'A lot of stamps have them.'

The manageress nodded. 'Yes, it is. And very hard to copy.' She held the forgery up again. 'As you can see, this watermark is far too blurred.'

'And those two checks together will detect pretty much any forgery,' said the police officer. 'Even a good one like this.'

'Pity we didn't check,' said Mr Hamilton.

The officer turned again to Peter's father. 'Exactly when did you give this note to Peter, Mr Hamilton?'

'Saturday morning,' said Peter's father. 'At about midday.'

'And can you say who gave it to you?'

'Well . . . no,' said Mr Hamilton.

'I see,' said the police officer. He jotted something down in his notebook.

'You don't think my dad's in on this, do you?' exploded Peter. 'He's no crook!'

Mr Hamilton put a hand on Peter's arm. 'Calm down, Peter. I'm sure the officer's not thinking any such thing.'

The policeman's face kept its serious look. 'So you think the note came into your possession at the car boot sale?' he said to Mr Hamilton.

'Possibly.'

'Possibly?'

'I went to the bank on Friday afternoon, and took out twenty pounds.'

The police officer's eyebrows rose. 'Are you suggesting that you received a counterfeit bank-note from a bank?'

'No . . . but I used that twenty-pound note when I bought my newspaper on the way to the boot sale on Saturday morning. What I'm saying is that I already had one ten-pound note in my pocket when I got there.'

'You definitely took another three at the car boot sale, Mr Hamilton,' said Holly.

'Did I?'

'You remember that, do you?' said the police officer to Holly.

'Oh, yes,' said Holly. 'We make it our business to remember things like that, don't we, Miranda?'

'Yes, we do,' Miranda said briskly. 'Before I went for a look around at the boot sale I saw Mr Hamilton take a ten-pound note from an elderly couple who bought his book-ends. She was a smart lady, called Ethel. Her husband's name was Horace. He had grey hair and was carrying one of those sticks you can spring out and sit on.'

'A shooting-stick,' said the police officer, impressed. He jotted down what Miranda had said in his notebook.

'And then there was the man who bought your engraving kit, Mr Hamilton,' said Holly. 'He gave you two ten-pound notes.'

Peter's father closed his eyes as he tried to conjure up the scene in his mind. 'I'm blowed if I can remember, Holly. It was all such a rush. But I don't doubt you're right.'

'He was smartly dressed too,' Holly said to the officer.

'Hold on,' said the officer, writing furiously, 'I can't keep up.'

'He was wearing a sports jacket and brown trousers. Oh, yes – and his shoes were really old.'

'Phew!' said the officer when he'd finished. 'Any more?'

'Were there any others, Mr Hamilton?' said Holly. 'I thought you had five ten-pound notes when you gave that one to Peter. You dropped them and I helped pick them up, remember? Counting the three we saw you take and the one you came with, that leaves one more.'

'Five?' said Mr Hamilton shaking his head. 'Did I?' He turned to the police officer. 'Sorry, I can't remember.'

'Hmm,' said the police officer. He closed his notebook. 'Very well. This looks like a genuine mistake. But if you do remember anything more, Mr Hamilton, you be sure to call us at the station – right?'

'Of course,' said Mr Hamilton.

The officer picked up the forged ten-pound note and slipped it into a plastic bag. 'In the meantime, I'm afraid, this is no use to you.'

As they all made to leave the manager's office, Peter picked up the shopping basket that he'd brought in with him from the check-out.

'Excuse me.' The manageress smiled kindly. 'You haven't paid for those goods yet, you know. And after all this I'm sure you wouldn't want to be accused of shoplifting.'

Peter gave an agonised look. 'But I haven't got any more money!'

Mr Hamilton sighed. 'How much?'

The manageress told him. Peter's father pulled out his wallet, then put it back again and dug into his trouser pocket instead.

'Why don't we pay with coins, eh? Be on the safe side.'

Straight after tea, Holly and Miranda met up and made their way round to Peter's house. This was where, in a tiny room between two bedrooms, the Mystery Kids had their 'office'.

They rang at the bell. After a few moments the door opened slightly. Peter peered out through the gap.

'Er . . . oh, hang on a minute.'

'Come on, Peter,' said Miranda. 'We've got a mystery to solve.' As Peter let the door go, she pushed it open.

'Oh, lovely!' cried Miranda. 'They really suit you!'

Peter was wearing an apron and a pair of bright-yellow rubber gloves.

'I'm in the middle of an experiment,' said Peter, looking slightly embarrassed. He led the way to the kitchen. On a cleared worktop they saw the familiar, battered orange box of Peter's chemistry set. Over on the hob, something was bubbling merrily in a saucepan.

'What are you doing?' asked Holly.

'At the moment, boiling red cabbage,' said Peter.

'I know I shouldn't ask this,' said Miranda, 'but – why?'

'Because the cabbage water is very useful.' He grinned as he picked up a small jar of purple liquid. 'This is some I prepared earlier.'

He poured some of the purple liquid into three saucers that he'd laid out on the worktop.

'You can use this stuff to test for acid.

Acid will turn the water from purple to red.'

'Acid?' said Holly. 'Isn't that dangerous?'

'Very strong acid is, yes,' said Peter. 'But not the sort I'm using.'

'What acid *are* you using then?' said Miranda, a little worried.

'Three sorts,' said Peter. Also on the worktop were the things he'd bought at the supermarket earlier. 'Citric acid, otherwise known as lemon juice,' he said, pointing at a small jug beside a squeezed lemon. 'Also tannic acid,' said Peter, pointing at another small jug of brown liquid, 'otherwise known as cold tea.' He poured some of the bottle of vinegar into a third jug, saying, 'And acetic acid.'

As they watched, Peter tipped a little of each of his acids into the three saucers of purple cabbage water. Instantly, each turned the water's colour from purple to red.

'There you are!' Peter said triumphantly. 'What do you think of that?'

'Impressive!' said Miranda. She rolled her eyes. 'Wouldn't a spoonful of strawberry jam do the same thing?'

'Is there more?' said Holly quickly. She'd

noticed that Peter had also set up a rack of three test-tubes, each with a small amount of dark-grey powder nestling at the bottom. 'Are they the famous iron-fillings?'

'Yes,' said Peter, with a quiet smile, 'they're for the second part of the experiment.'

This time he carefully poured some lemon juice into one of the tubes of iron-filings, some cold tea into another, and some vinegar into the third. He stood back and watched as the contents of the three test-tubes just sat there.

'What now?' yawned Miranda.

'We leave them.'

'For how long?' asked Holly.

'Ah. That's the experiment. I'm not sure how long it will take to work. At least an hour, I think; maybe longer.'

'Work?' said Miranda. 'How do you mean, work? It won't explode? I don't fancy being the first schoolgirl in space.'

'No, it's perfectly safe,' said Peter. 'Explode is what it's *not* going to do.'

'What is it going to do then?' asked Holly.

'Wait and see,' grinned Peter. 'Come on, let's go up to the office, shall we?'

'Er . . . before we go,' called Miranda as

Peter headed for the stairs, 'can we try one more experiment?'

'Of course,' said Peter. 'I didn't think you liked science, Miranda. What sort of experiment?'

'I call it my hot chocolate experiment,' said Miranda. 'It always works. You heat up some milk, put this powdery stuff called chocolate on top of it, stir it round and round until it dissolves and bingo – you've made a drink!'

Peter couldn't help laughing. 'OK, I can take a hint. The hot chocolate experiment it is, then. But I'll have to use the hob for heating the milk. When we found my chemistry set, the bunsen burner was missing, remember.'

Clutching their mugs of steaming chocolate, the Mystery Kids headed up the stairs and into their office. It was just a small box-room, with one little window, but large enough to take a chair and a small table. On the wall was a huge map of London. At its side was a little group of coloured marker pins.

Holly went straight over to the board and stuck a red pin into the map. Red for mystery.

'Thomas Petheridge Comprehensive School,' she announced.

'The case of the funny money,' said Miranda. 'Sounds like a new file, Holly.'

Holly pulled her notebook out of her bag. She picked up her pen. Each of the Mystery Kids had a real police notebook, given to them when they caught a pair of jewel thieves.

'The investigation starts here. So – what do we know?'

'Somebody is passing fake ten-pound notes,' said Peter. 'At car boot sales.'

'Hmm. We don't know for certain that's where your dad got it,' said Holly.

'But it's pretty likely, isn't it?' said Miranda.

Holly nodded. 'Likely location,' she wrote, 'Thomas Petheridge School.' She looked at Peter and Miranda. 'So, what can we remember about the people who came to our table?'

'There's the elderly couple Miranda told the police officer about,' said Peter. 'That was a brilliant description.'

'Horace and Ethel,' said Holly. 'They don't sound like crooks.'

'Ever heard of Bonnie and Clyde?' said

Miranda. She aimed both her index fingers. 'K-pow, k-pow! Shooting up America in an orgy of blood and bullets.'

'They were in their twenties, weren't they?' said Peter. 'Horace and Ethel must have been over sixty!'

'So they're late developers,' said Miranda. 'And who would suspect them, eh? Innocent-looking old folk like them.'

'I'll put them down,' said Holly, doing so. 'Now, how about Mr Sports Jacket? The man who bought your dad's engraving kit, Peter.'

'I didn't see him,' said Miranda. 'I was haggling over my props by then.'

'The ten-pound notes he paid with were quite new, just like the one your dad gave you, Peter. And he was very smartly dressed. Apart from his shoes,' added Holly. 'They were really old.'

'How does all that lot fit together?' said Miranda.

Holly looked thoughtful. 'I don't know. But do people come to boot sales smartly dressed? Could he have just been trying to create a good impression?'

'Why?' said Peter.

Holly shrugged. 'Because – well, right or wrong, scruffy people do *look* more suspicious, don't they?'

'Could be,' said Peter.

'Bonnie and Clyde were natty dressers,' said Miranda, sipping her hot chocolate. 'Until they got riddled with bullets, that is.'

'Thank you, Miranda!' said Holly. She turned to Peter. 'Has your dad remembered who gave him the fourth ten-pound note?'

'No,' said Peter absently.

He got to his feet, went to the door and looked out. 'Can you smell anything?'

Holly and Miranda shook their heads. 'Only chocolate,' said Miranda. 'Very nice, too.'

Peter returned to his chair. 'What do we do now?'

'Check out our suspects?' said Miranda. 'What do you think, Holly?'

'Definitely. I think we need to keep watch on the car boot sale next Saturday.'

'Won't the police be doing that, after what we told them?' Peter said.

'Possibly,' said Holly. 'But there's no reason why we shouldn't keep watch too. And if we do spot our suspects, we can tell the police at once.'

'It won't be easy spotting them,' said Peter. 'It was pretty crowded, wasn't it?' He gave another glance towards the door. 'Are you sure you can't smell anything?'

'If we waited at the gate,' suggested Holly, 'we could look for them in the queue, then follow them around from there.'

'What we really need is John Raven's helicopter,' said Miranda. 'Remember last week?'

The previous week's episode of *Spyglass* was still fresh in Holly's mind. Secret Agent John Raven had commandeered a helicopter in his chase of a suspect. 'I like the idea, Miranda,' she laughed. 'Any idea where we'd get hold of one?'

'Look in the *Yellow Pages*?'

'We don't need a helicopter,' said Peter, absently. 'We just need to be at the top of a high building.'

'The drama room!' cried Holly. 'We could keep a lookout from up there on Saturday morning!'

'We'd need permission,' said Miranda. 'Maybe we could ask if we can rehearse our mystery sketch.'

'Brilliant! That way we'll see everybody who comes in.'

Holly rapidly drew a plan of the school on a fresh sheet of paper. Then, pinning it to the corner of their notice-board, she attached it to a short length of white tape which ended at the red pin marking their school. On Holly's plan, a large cross marked the building in which the drama room was situated. Arrows ran out from there in all directions.

'There's virtually no part of the boot sale area we won't be able to see,' she said, excitedly. 'Well done, Peter.'

But Peter wasn't paying attention. He was looking over towards the door. 'Are you sure you can't smell anything?'

Miranda twitched her nose, sniffed doubtfully at the cup, then twitched her nose again. 'Ye-es,' she said. 'Now you come to mention it – yes, I can.'

Holly did the same. There definitely was something in the air. 'So can I,' she said. 'And it's horrible.'

'It's not only horrible,' said Miranda. 'It's getting stronger.'

Peter frowned. 'It's not supposed to do that,' he said.

'What isn't?' said Holly.

'My experiment,' said Peter.

'Well, it's done it,' Miranda yelled as the smell suddenly got a whole lot worse. 'Let me out!'

They thundered down the stairs and into the kitchen, the awful smell getting stronger by the second.

'Oh, no!' yelled Peter.

Sitting on the worktop, next to the bright-red hob, the mixtures in Peter's three test-tubes were bubbling and foaming . . . and stinking. Pausing only to grab three corks, Peter snatched up the test-tube rack. 'Stand back!' he shouted.

'Gladly!' mumbled Miranda, her nose covered by a handkerchief.

Holly opened the back door. Peter hurtled through it, holding the test-tube rack with one hand and his nose with the other.

The two girls jumped out into the garden themselves, breathing in lungfuls of fresh air.

'Where have you put them?' asked Holly when Peter returned.

'At the bottom of the garden.'

'Not far enough,' said Miranda.

'In the shed,' said Peter.

'It'll get out through the cracks,' said Miranda, tying her handkerchief round her nose like a bandit out of a cowboy film.

'In a metal box,' added Peter. 'In the saddlebag of my bike.'

'OK,' said Miranda. 'We stand a chance.'

'What happened?' asked Holly.

'I forgot to turn the hob off after making our drinks,' said Peter. 'The test-tubes were next to it, and the mixtures must have got hot.'

Miranda lifted her handkerchief for just long enough to say, 'What a disaster!'

Peter clearly thought otherwise. Slowly his face creased into the most enormous grin. 'Disaster? What are you talking about? It was brilliant! I thought it would work, but nothing like as well as that!'

'Work?' said Holly. 'That experiment worked?'

'Not half,' grinned Peter. 'It was a stink-bomb experiment. We learned in Science that if you mixed iron and acid you'd get a bit of a pong. I wanted to see which would give me the best.'

'The worst, you mean,' said Holly.

'Right,' laughed Peter. 'But I didn't know that heating them up did that!'

He was still chuckling to himself as a bellow came from the house.

'Peter!!'

'My dad! He must have come home!'

They ran back into the kitchen to find Mr Hamilton standing there. He'd opened every window and turned the extractor fan on full blast.

'I thought I'd sold that!' he yelled, pointing to Peter's chemistry set box on the worktop.

Peter looked flustered. 'We found it again. In one of the school rubbish bins.'

Mr Hamilton looked as though he was going to say something. Then, suddenly, he spun on his heel and strode into the hallway.

'What are you doing?' asked Peter.

'Just calling the police,' said Mr Hamilton, picking up the phone.

'The police?' said Holly.

'The police?' echoed Miranda. 'Not the fire brigade?'

'What for?' said Peter. 'There's nothing wrong. It was just an experiment. The smell will go away soon.'

'You can apologise later,' said Mr Hamilton,

71

'because, I've just remembered who gave me that other ten-pound note.'

'You have? Who?'

'The man who bought your chemistry set.'

5 On the lookout

'Phew!' gasped Miranda. 'At last! The things I do for the Mystery Kids!'

Elbowing her way into the drama room, she plonked the suitcase down in the middle of the floor.

'I'm not sure why you brought all that stuff,' Holly said as Miranda collapsed on to the case, gasping dramatically for breath. 'I mean, we aren't actually going to rehearse, are we?'

'Call yourself a mystery fan,' tutted Miranda, recovering miraculously. 'Haven't you ever heard of cover? Anybody spying on us spying on them will see us with this lot on and decide we're not spying on them after all, won't they?'

'On?' said Peter. 'Did you say *on*?'

'Yes, on,' repeated Miranda. 'As in "put on".' She clicked open the suitcase. 'OK, who wants what?'

'Can we have a look and see what's going on first, Miranda?' said Holly.

She moved across to look out of the drama room window. Peter came to stand beside her. It was just before ten o'clock and out by the main school gate the usual long queue had formed. They watched a small blue van edge its way through the gate and over to the far corner of the grounds.

'That one's cutting it a bit fine,' said Peter. He looked at his watch. 'They'll be letting the buyers in any minute now.'

Miranda joined them. 'So we're looking for Horace and Ethel,' she said. 'And Mr Sports Jacket.'

'And the unknown chemistry-set buyer,' said Peter.

Holly looked at him. 'It's a pity your dad couldn't remember what he looked like,' she said.

'Yes,' said Peter. 'He just vaguely remembered that it was a man.'

Miranda looked down on the scene below. 'Any sign of our other suspects, Holly? Holly?'

Beside her, Holly had stopped gazing out of the window. She had turned away in thought. Suddenly she turned back.

74

'We don't want the others,' she said urgently. 'We want the man who bought your chemistry set. *He*'s the one!'

'How do you make that out?' said Peter.

Holly's eyes were gleaming. 'If you were trying to pass off forged bank-notes, what would you do?'

'Use them to buy something valuable with,' said Peter after a few moments' thought. 'You're getting something for nothing, remember.'

'But then you'd have to sell it again to get the money. And what can you get that's really valuable for ten pounds, anyway?'

'Not a lot.'

'So,' said Holly, 'why not do the opposite?'

'What?'

'Buy small things. Things that don't cost much.'

'I get it,' said Peter. 'You buy something for two pounds, hand over a ten-pound note . . .'

'And get eight pounds in *good* money as change. That's what he was doing!'

'OK,' said Peter, 'but then what? He ends up with a sackful of good change but a load of junk he doesn't want.'

'Like your chemistry set!' said Miranda.

'That is not junk,' said Peter.

'I didn't mean it that way,' said Miranda. 'But if he just bought it as a way of passing that fake ten-pound note to your dad then he wouldn't want it, would he?'

'And that's why he threw it away! That's why it was in the school rubbish bin!'

'Holly, that's brilliant!'

Holly turned again to the window. 'So we can forget Sports Jacket, and Ethel and Horace. We're looking for somebody . . .'

Peter finished the sentence for her. 'But we don't know who. It's not going to be easy.'

They'd been watching without success for just over half an hour when, along the silent corridor, they heard a door close.

'What was that?' said Holly.

They listened hard. Another door opened, then closed. Heavy footsteps came their way, then stopped.

'More to the point,' said Miranda, *who* is that?'

Another door opened. The footsteps, slow and steady, were on the other side of the wall now.

76

'Powell!' said Holly.

'The caretaker?' said Peter.

'It must be. He's on his rounds, checking the building.'

'So, we'll be on his list, won't we? We've got permission to be in here.'

'Yes,' said Holly. 'Rehearsing! Not on the lookout for people passing fake money!'

'What shall we do?'

'Take cover, of course!' said Miranda, dashing over to her suitcase. 'Come on, quick! Get these on!'

She began firing props in all directions. 'Peter, you put the trench coat on. Holly, you have the bowler hat and the cigarette holder. I'll have the glasses, moustache and nose.'

No sooner had they put the things on than the door opened. Powell, the school caretaker, stepped slowly into the room. He was wearing a brown coat and had a clipboard in his hand.

'Names?' he said solemnly.

Holly took the cigarette holder out of her mouth. 'Holly Adams, Miranda Hunt and Peter Hamilton,' she said briskly.

'Rehearsing,' said Peter, twirling round in his long coat.

'Drama,' added Miranda, scratching her false nose.

'For the school talent contest,' said Holly. She dipped into her bag and pulled out the three tickets she'd bought for her mother, father and brother Jamie only the day before.

Powell looked at them, sniffed, then slowly ticked the sheet of paper attached to his clipboard.

The three friends waited for him to move. But he didn't. Instead of heading for the door, he settled himself on the edge of a desk.

'Don't mind me. I like a good play.'

'Er . . . oh,' said Holly. 'Right, then. Er . . . Miranda?'

'Holly?' said Miranda, moving closer.

'Peter?' said Miranda, beckoning him near.

'What are we going to do?' Holly whispered as the three of them got into a huddle.

'Scream?' hissed Miranda. 'How about if I just scream?'

'Why not do your mystery act?' whispered Peter. He turned to look at the caretaker. Powell was drumming his fingers impatiently on his clipboard.

'Good thinking, Peter,' said Miranda. 'Holly,

we'll do our Holmes and Watson bit on Powell.'

'I suppose we could,' said Holly. 'With luck he'll go away in a minute.'

'Right,' said Miranda.

'And at least that way Peter can keep watching.'

'Come on, come on,' called Powell. 'If I was a proper audience I'd be chucking tomatoes by now.'

Holly swallowed hard. 'OK,' she said. 'Here goes.'

She stepped back. 'Ready, Watson?' she said loudly to Miranda.

'Ready, Holmes,' said Miranda.

As Peter wandered back over to the window, Holly and Miranda walked slowly towards the caretaker. They stopped in front of him, looking him up and down.

'Watson?' said Holly.

Miranda adjusted her glasses and twitched her moustache.

'Yes, Holmes?'

'We have a problem on our hands.'

'You can say that again,' said Miranda.

Holly shook her head, holding the bowler hat on with one hand as it almost fell off. 'No,

79

no. What I mean is, that we have to deduce what we can about this man purely from the evidence of our eyes.'

'Tricky, Holmes, tricky. But if anybody can, you can.'

Holly adjusted her cigarette holder. She turned her head this way and that as she stood in front of the caretaker.

'To begin, Watson. Note the tear in the right-hand sleeve of his brown coat.'

Powell's eyes flickered uncertainly down to his sleeve.

Miranda jiggled her false spectacles. 'I see it, Holmes. But what does it tell us?'

'That he carries his knife and fork in a very strange place,' said Holly.

She paced backwards and forwards for a moment, then stopped. She looked at the caretaker's coat again.

'Then how about that stain, Watson?'

Again, Powell looked down uncertainly at the damp patch on the left-hand side of his brown coat.

'Blood?' said Miranda, wide-eyed. 'Could it be blood?'

'Possibly, possibly,' said Holly.

Miranda pulled her false nose out and let it

spring back with a *thwack*. 'I have it, Holmes! He's just bumped off the headmaster!'

'With the knife he keeps up his sleeve!' cried Holly. 'I see it all!'

'What you see,' growled Powell, looking from Holly to Miranda and back again, 'is a sleeve what got caught on my door handle, causing me to spill my tea all over myself. That's what you see.'

Holly almost burst out laughing. The only thing that stopped her was another voice, coming suddenly from behind her.

'Excuse me, Mr Holmes, Dr Watson. There is something very suspicious going on round here.'

Holly whirled round. It was Peter. He was joining in!

'Er . . . pardon?' she stammered.

'*Very* suspicious,' repeated Peter, rolling his eyes over towards the window.

'Who are you?' asked Miranda in her deepest Dr Watson voice.

'A person who has been keeping watch on events,' said Peter loudly, 'and has seen some suspicious goings-on.'

'I see,' said Holly. But she didn't see at all. What was Peter doing?

Suddenly, Holly realised. He must have spotted something suspicious going on at the car boot sale!

'Oh, I *see!*'

But Peter was already striding towards the drama room door. 'You must come at once, Mr Holmes! Follow me, if you please.'

'At once!' cried Holly. She gestured madly to Miranda. 'Come, Watson! Let us investigate this man's evidence a little further.'

Miranda put her hands on her hips. 'What?'

Holly was at the door. 'Come on, Watson!'

'OK!' yelled Miranda, finally realising what Holly and Peter were doing. 'Right behind you, Holmes!'

As they all dashed out of the drama room, Powell the caretaker shook his head slowly.

'What a load of rubbish!' he cried.

They scurried down the stairs. Peter stopped as they reached the landing on the floor below. They were able to see out into the carpark from there.

'Have you seen something?' asked Holly.

'I'm not sure,' said Peter. He pointed. 'But,

look. Over there. See that blue van we saw coming in earlier?'

'Yes.'

'Well, it's just been sitting there.'

'So what's suspicious about that?' said Miranda. 'It was there last week as well.'

'It was?' Peter looked out at the van.

'All the time I was haggling with my amateur dramatics lady,' said Miranda. 'There was a man with a shoe-lace tie sitting in it all the time. You asked me if I'd bought my props from him; don't you remember, Holly?'

Holly nodded.

'But you don't bring a car into a boot sale just to sit in it, do you?' said Peter. 'It should have its doors open like all the other cars, and somebody at the back of it, selling things. Don't you think that's suspicious?'

'Why should it be?' said Miranda. 'People do come to boot sales just to buy, don't they?'

'But then they don't bring their car in!' cried Holly. 'Is that what you're saying, Peter?'

'Yes,' said Peter. 'It costs far more to bring

a car in. So why do it if you're not selling anything?'

They all looked out of the landing window again. The blue van was still sitting in its spot, with no signs of activity at all. Suddenly, a man climbed out of the passenger seat and walked away – a tall man, with a long-sleeved shirt and a shoe-lace tie.

'There he goes!' said Holly.

'What do we do now?' said Miranda. 'Follow him?'

'Look in the van,' said Peter.

Holly said, 'Why don't we look in the van first, while he's not there? That way, if we spot anything suspicious we'll know it's worth following him.'

Miranda and Peter seemed undecided, until the heavy footsteps of Powell the caretaker sounded on the floor above.

'Agreed!' yelled Miranda.

Moments later they were pushing their way through the swing doors and out into the milling crowds.

'What if he spots us?' asked Peter.

'In this crowd?' said Miranda. 'I think we're safe.'

*　　*　　*

They made their way towards the van. Even from where they were they could see that it was quite old. One of its wings was rusty, as were the bottoms of both of its rear doors. The only thing about the van that seemed to be new was a gleaming lightning-bolt logo painted on its side panel.

Holly led the way. 'We need to look in the back,' she said as they threaded their way through the crowds to within twenty metres of the van. 'If there are lots of little things there—'

She broke off in mid-sentence as, a little way ahead, the van's door suddenly opened.

Holly gasped. 'Oh, no! Shoe-lace has got somebody with him!'

'He must have been sitting in the driver's seat all along,' said Peter, stopping beside her.

Over by the van, the driver had got out. He was a short, stocky man with crew-cut hair. Stuffing his hands into the pockets of his faded jeans, he'd begun to look around. Now he was staring – at them!

'He's spotted us!' said Miranda. 'How?'

Holly almost burst out laughing. 'Probably

because you don't often see a twelve-year-old girl with a black moustache, Miranda. We're all still in our stage gear!'

'Well, that's it,' said Peter. 'We're not going to get a look in that van now, are we?'

'Why not?' It was Miranda.

'Miranda, he's seen us,' said Holly. The man was still looking their way.

'He may have seen us, but he hasn't seen *us*. He doesn't *know* we want to sneak a look in the back of his van, does he?'

'I suppose not.'

'Of course not. And there's three of us. If you and I keep him occupied, Peter could take a look, couldn't he?'

'I could,' said Peter.

'But how are we going to keep him occupied?' said Holly.

Miranda twirled the end of her moustache. 'Just get those talent contest tickets out – and come with me.'

Arms looped, the two girls strolled towards the van.

'Are you sure this is going to work?' Holly whispered out of the corner of her mouth.

'No,' said Miranda. 'But it's too late now. He knows we're coming.'

Ahead of them, the van driver was looking straight at them. And he wasn't smiling.

'Excuse me, sir,' said Miranda as they stopped in front of him.

'What do you want?' said the man. His eyes flicked from Miranda to Holly and back again.

Miranda pointed to the tickets in Holly's hand. 'Interest you in buying a ticket, can we?' trilled Miranda. 'The school talent show. Lots of wonderful acts. Like – well, us for a start.'

The man shook his head. 'No,' he said gruffly.

Out of the corner of her eye, Holly could see Peter creeping closer to the back of the van. They had to keep this man's attention for a bit longer.

'Not even one?' she said to the driver. 'They're only two pounds each.'

'Two for three pounds,' Miranda said brightly. 'You could bring your mum.'

'I said no. Now clear off!'

Not much longer, thought Holly. Peter must be at the back of the van by now.

They only needed to keep his attention for a few seconds longer.

'Are you sure?' said Holly. 'It's all in aid of school funds.'

'To buy us poor schoolkids those little essentials,' said Miranda, sniffling. 'Like pencils. I'm down to my last one . . .'

With a grunt of annoyance, the man pulled a hand out of the pocket of his faded jeans. In it was a roll of ten-pound notes!

Holly gasped. Were they forgeries? If they could get hold of one and take it to the police – that would be real evidence!

The man was peeling a note from the roll. He was holding it out to Miranda . . .

'*Hey!!*'

As the loud bellow reached their ears, Holly swung round. Racing towards them, his shoe-lace tie flapping as he ran, was the man they'd seen earlier. As he got closer she could see that he was much taller than the driver, with much longer fair hair.

'What do you think you're doing?'

Before Holly could say anything, she heard Peter's voice. The man had been shouting at Peter, not at them.

'Just looking,' said Peter, casually strolling

away from the back of the van. 'I collect car numbers. It's a hobby of mine.'

Shoe-lace was in no mood for messing around. 'Clear off,' he yelled to Peter. Then, to his mate, 'What do you think you're doing? Are you mad? Put that lot away.'

Yanking open the passenger door, Shoe-lace jumped into the van. The driver hastily put his roll of bank-notes back into his pocket and snatched open the driver's door.

Moments later the van reversed out of its spot and threaded its way towards the main gates.

'Did you see that pile of bank-notes?' said Miranda, whistling. 'Do you think they were all funny money?'

'I don't know,' said Holly. 'Gosh, it's a pity we didn't get hold of one. That would have told us if we were right.'

'I'm certain we *are* right,' said Peter. He'd found a scrap of paper in the pocket of the trench coat and was jotting down the van's number.

Holly looked at him. 'Why? Did you see something?'

Peter nodded. 'In the back of the van.'

'What?'

'My missing bunsen burner.' He looked over to where the van was accelerating fiercely down the road. 'One of those two must have been the person who bought my old chemistry set.'

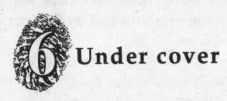

6 Under cover

They went straight round to Peter's house. Armed with glasses of orange juice and a plateful of biscuits, the Mystery Kids were soon in their office and deep in thought.

'What do we do now?' said Holly.

'Go to the police?' suggested Miranda, uncertainly.

Peter shook his head slowly. 'I don't think we've got enough, have we?'

'We could tell them about your chemistry set, and how we suspect Shoe-lace gave your dad that fake ten-pound note when he bought it.'

'But we can't *prove* it, can we?' said Peter.

'How about the number of that van of theirs?' said Miranda.

'What about it?'

'You're the car number plates expert, Peter,' said Miranda.

She waved an arm towards a bookshelf sagging under the weight of a number of large binders. 'If we went to the police and told them that number, couldn't they find out who those men were?'

Peter thought about this. When he'd told the man at the boot sale he collected car numbers he hadn't been lying. It really *was* Peter's hobby and he had masses of information on the subject. Whilst Miranda and Holly couldn't understand the fascination of the subject for anybody, it had certainly been useful in the past.

'Yes,' said Peter, finally. 'They could contact the Licensing Centre. But I think they'd only do that if we had some proof. Even then, they'd only be able to trace those men if one of them actually owns the van,' said Peter. 'They may not. That lightning-bolt logo it had on the side makes me think it's a company van.'

'A company van?' said Holly, sucking the end of her pencil thoughtfully. 'What sort of company?'

'Electronics?' said Peter.

'How about a locksmith?' said Miranda. She gave a snort of laughter. 'They might have the slogan: "We sell the most powerful bolts in the business!"'

Holly's mind was on other things. 'No,' she said. 'What I meant was, why didn't that van have the name of the company on the side? They usually do, don't they? There's the name and the telephone number.'

'Sort of free advertising,' said Peter. 'You're right, Holly.'

'Maybe they don't want to advertise themselves,' said Miranda.

'But that would be daft,' said Holly. 'If companies don't advertise, they don't get any business. What sort of company is it that doesn't want business?'

She suddenly looked at the others, her eyes gleaming. 'A fake company, that's who!'

Peter looked at her. 'Fake? You mean one that doesn't actually do any business?'

'But – why?' said Miranda.

'Miranda, because they're not just passing the money – they're making it as well!'

'Why go to all the trouble of setting up a business, though?'

'So that they don't arouse any suspicion,' said Holly. Another thought occurred to her. 'That logo, Peter. Didn't it look new?'

Peter nodded. 'Yes, it did. Much newer than the van. From the first letter on its number plate, it was nearly ten years old.'

'You could tell that from the rust,' said Miranda.

Holly steepled her fingers under her chin. 'Doesn't that fit, too? A fake business wouldn't need a new van, would they? They'd buy a cheap old one.'

Peter and Miranda nodded in agreement. 'Sounds good,' said Peter.

'So where does it get us?' asked Miranda. 'What do we do now?'

'Track down that van,' said Holly.

'What!' cried Miranda. She tapped on their wall map of London. 'In case it's escaped your notice, Holly, London is a pretty big place. Finding that van could take us forever.'

'There must be some way of narrowing the search.'

'How?' said Miranda. 'We don't know the name of the company, so we can't look them up in the *Yellow Pages*. All we have is the number plate of their van – and Peter says the only way of finding out more about that is to go to the police.'

'So we'll just have to wait until next week's

boot sale,' Holly said. 'And hope we see it again.'

She looked at Peter's bookshelves, sagging with binders full of information about car number plates he'd collected.

'Peter,' she said, 'is there any chance that *you've* seen that van before?'

Peter glanced up at his binders as Holly went on. 'I mean, if you had, would it help?'

'Well – yes, a bit,' said Peter. 'I make a note of where I am when I see a number plate . . .'

'Holly,' said Miranda, puffing out her cheeks. 'Look at the *size* of those binders. Finding a number plate in that lot has got to be even harder than finding the van itself!'

Peter stood up. He was shaking his head and smiling. 'Now there you're wrong, Miranda. I can check if I've seen it very quickly.' He headed for the door. 'It's a long shot, though. Come on.'

Holly and Miranda followed Peter downstairs to the small back room Mr Hamilton used as a study.

'A computer?' said Holly as Peter turned on the machine on Mr Hamilton's desk.

The computer whined and clicked as it

powered up. 'Yes. I've been setting up a database on it.'

'You mean . . .' began Miranda.

Peter grinned. 'Have I got all my car numbers stored on it? Yes, I have.'

As the screen display came alive, Peter tapped in a command from the keyboard. 'This is my number plate analysis program,' he said as the display changed.

'Keep it simple, Peter,' Miranda said quickly. 'Just find the number, eh?'

Peter tapped a few more keys. On the screen a question flashed up: 'NUMBER PLATE WANTED?' Carefully he typed in the number of the van.

Almost instantly the answer came back. 'SEEN ON 18TH MARCH. REFERENCE F-242.'

'Seen?' said Holly. 'You have seen it before? Where?'

'Ah,' said Peter, exiting the program and turning off the computer, 'for that we have to go back to good old paper. I don't type everything into the computer. It takes too long. That's what the reference number is. It tells me which of my binders I've got the details in.'

'All go, isn't it, Holly?' said Miranda as they followed Peter back up to the office again.

There, Peter reached up and pulled a ring binder from the shelf. 'F registration numbers,' he said, indicating the large 'F' on the binder's spine. 'Now to have a look at entry 242.'

Holly and Miranda looked on as he flipped through the pages. Each was divided up into columns, with headings such as date, type of car, colour and where seen.

'Ah!' said Peter. 'Got it. "Monday the 18th March, between five and six pm".'

'Where did you see it?' Holly asked eagerly. This could be the break they needed. 'Near here?'

Peter ran his finger across the page to the 'where seen' column – and gave an embarrassed cough. 'Er . . . well . . . it's good news and bad news.'

'Let's have the bad news first,' said Miranda.

'The bad news is that I've only written "Highgate",' said Peter. 'I usually put more than that. I must have been in a hurry that day . . .'

'Highgate,' said Miranda, shaking her head.

'That's *really* helpful. That narrows it down a lot.'

'How about the good news?' said Holly.

Peter closed the ring binder. 'The good news is that I only have three watching spots in Highgate.'

Holly signalled and pulled into the kerb. Behind her, Peter and Miranda did the same.

'When I want to cycle around all Sunday afternoon,' gasped Miranda, 'I'll enter the *Tour de France*.'

'I never knew there were so many roads in Highgate,' said Holly.

'Or hills,' moaned Miranda, leaning her head on her handlebars. She looked up. 'And what have we seen? Plenty of blue vans, but not one of them with a lightning bolt. Oh, yes – and one lightning bolt without a blue van.'

'Where was that?' said Peter.

'Halfway up a pylon, warning people not to climb it,' said Miranda, letting her head fall back on her handlebars again.

They'd been to the first two watching spots that Peter had used. Both times they'd started from the spot and cycled the roads all around it, looking for any trace of the blue van.

The first, quite close to Thomas Petheridge School, had taken them a long time. The roads around the school were quite short, but there had been many of them. The second spot, at the bottom of Highgate Hill, had been almost as bad. There had been fewer roads to examine, but they'd all seemed to be going uphill.

Peter pointed a little way ahead. 'That's the only other spot I've used.'

Dismounting from her bike, Holly wound the pedals round so that it was standing securely against the kerb. She looked at the spot Peter had indicated, then back at him.

Was there a better way of tackling this problem? What deductions would Sherlock Holmes have made?

An idea came to her.

'Why?' she said.

Peter frowned. 'Why what?'

'Why there? Why not further down. Or back that way?'

'Or outside your front gate?' mumbled Miranda, head down. 'Sitting in a deckchair, with a nice cool drink.'

'Because of the lights,' said Peter, pointing at the set of traffic lights not far away. 'They make the traffic stop regularly. That way I have time to write the numbers down.'

'There are lots of places with traffic lights, Peter. Why here?'

'Because this is a crossroads,' said Peter. 'This road we're on leads out of Highgate to the north, and into Central London to the south.' He pointed off to the right. 'And that one runs east to the main shopping area.'

'So there's lots of traffic to see here?' said Holly.

'Right,' said Peter. 'I want to collect as many numbers as I can, remember. There's no point in choosing somewhere quiet.'

Holly thought hard. This didn't seem to be getting them very far. Was there anything she'd missed? What else did they know?

'The time, Peter. Why would you have come here between five and six pm?'

'I told you,' said Peter. 'I want to get as many numbers as possible. That's the rush hour. There's more traffic at that time.'

'Heading out of London?'

'Yes. And out from the industrial estate,' he said, pointing away to the left.

Holly looked at him. 'The industrial estate?' she said slowly.

Miranda lifted her head from her handlebars. 'As in lots of companies . . .'

'And lots of company vans,' said Holly. 'It's worth a try.'

The industrial estate was like a housing estate except that, instead of houses, there were rows of small factories and workshops. They ranged in size from the fairly large, to others that were small and bleak. Each had a name above its entrance. Some had a logo.

Holly, Peter and Miranda cycled slowly along, looking either for the van itself or for any sign of its lightning-bolt logo.

'That's the lot,' said Peter as they cycled into the short, final road.

'Nothing,' said Miranda, drawing to a halt beside him. 'Not a sausage. Or a lightning-bolt.'

'I was sure we'd find something,' said Holly. 'Sure of it.'

She looked round helplessly. On both sides of the road, buildings were closed and shuttered for the weekend. Only a dull, clanking noise coming from somewhere indicated that the area wasn't completely deserted.

Holly sighed. Ahead of them was a small furniture warehouse, then the offices of a security firm. After that, the road seemed to peter out into an area of waste ground edged by trees and overgrown shrubbery. They'd drawn a blank.

'Quiet, isn't it?' said Miranda, from beside her.

'It *is* Sunday,' said Peter.

Holly said, 'If it wasn't for that clanking, I'd think the whole place was a ghost town!'

She listened carefully. The noise appeared to be coming from somewhere ahead of them.

But it *didn't* seem to be coming from either of the two buildings she could see. Rather, it seemed to be coming from beyond them – from close by the trees.

Holly pedalled slowly on, past the offices and past the warehouse. Tucked away in the corner opposite the waste ground, she saw a small grey building with a signboard above its entrance.

'There it is!'

In the corner of the signboard was a lightning-bolt logo.

'"Speedi-Print",' said Peter, reading the board. '"We Print Like Lightning"'

'A printers!' said Miranda. 'Holly, you could be right. They *could* actually be making those fake bank-notes – here!'

'A printing machine,' said Peter. 'I bet that's what's making the noise!' The rhythmic clanking sounds grew louder as they got nearer. It seemed to be coming from behind the building.

'The perfect disguise,' said Holly. 'Nobody would think it strange to hear sounds of printing equipment working.'

'Is printing equipment noisy?' said Miranda. 'The school photocopier is pretty quiet.'

'A real printing press isn't, though,' said Peter.

Suddenly the clanking stopped.

Holly's mind was made up. 'We need to look round the back,' she said urgently.

'What for?' said Miranda. 'You don't expect to see packing cases marked "money", do you?'

'I don't know, Miranda. That's why we're looking. Their van might be there for a start.'

Quickly they cycled over to the cover of the trees.

'I've brought my camera with me,' said Peter. 'We could get some interesting pictures.'

As they dismounted, Peter opened the top flap of his saddle-bag.

'Well, whatever you do, don't open *that*!' said Miranda.

In the saddle-bag, alongside his puncture repair kit, was the metal tin into which Peter had hurriedly shoved his test-tube rack after his chemistry experiment.

Holly agreed. 'Miranda's right, Peter. We want to photograph them. Not gas them!'

Peter took his camera from the saddle-bag and let the flap down again.

Taking his camera out of its case, Peter leaned cautiously out from the trees. Checking that it was all clear, he took a couple of shots of the front door and the Speedi-Print sign.

'It won't be easy getting round the back,' he said when he'd finished.

A driveway ran along the far side of the building, clearly designed so that delivery vehicles could get round to the back. But it was very open and there was no way the Mystery Kids could get close to the building without being seen.

'Look!' said Holly. 'There! We can go that way!'

The near side of the building ended just before the line of the trees. Between the two, shrouded by overhanging branches, Holly had spotted a narrow alleyway.

'How about if I keep a lookout while you two go and take some pictures?' said Miranda.

'Are you sure?' said Holly.

'Sure I'm sure. You know me and cameras. If I so much as breathe near one it stops working.'

Swiftly, Holly and Peter ran alongside the trees. Moments later they were in the alley and scuttling alongside the Speedi-Print building. Moments after that, they discovered a flaw in their plan.

Where the building ended, a high wall began – and continued all the way along until it reached a dead-end.

'There must be a loading area on the other side of this wall,' whispered Peter as they inched their way back again.

They stopped to listen. The machine noise hadn't started up again. All was quiet.

'It doesn't sound as though much is going on,' said Peter.

As if to prove him wrong, at that very moment, on the other side of the wall, they heard the squeal of tyres as something raced into the loading area and screeched to a halt. More sounds followed – of doors opening, and running feet.

And then they heard Miranda. She was running, too – down the alleyway towards them.

'The van,' she gasped. '*The* van. It's here. It just came roaring in like it was in a Grand Prix race.'

'Who was driving?' asked Peter.

Miranda shook her head wildly. 'I couldn't tell. It came in too fast.'

On the other side of the wall something was definitely happening. Feet were hurrying. And a man's voice, cold and precise, was saying, 'Fifteen seconds.'

'We have to take some pictures,' said Holly. She looked up at the top of the wall. 'Quick, Peter. Give me a leg up.'

'You're not going over?'

Holly pointed to the branches above their heads, and the thick tree trunk on the other side of the wall.

'I can hide behind the tree. They won't see me.'

'Thirty seconds,' called the voice.

Peter put his hands together to form a stirrup. Putting her foot into them, Holly clambered up to the top of the wall – and over.

'Now me,' said Miranda.

'It doesn't need two,' said Peter.

'No?' said Miranda. She pointed to the small grey case that Peter had put on the ground before helping Holly over the wall. 'It does if the first one has forgotten to take the camera with her.'

Moments later, Miranda was clambering over the wall to drop down on the other side.

'How about this?' she whispered, handing Holly the camera.

Holly looked serious. 'I don't think it's going to help. We can't see a thing!'

They'd landed beside the thick tree trunk. But also in the middle of an overgrown clump of shrubbery that they hadn't been able to see from the other side of the wall.

'Surrounded,' groaned Miranda as she looked from side to side. 'The only way out of here is back over the wall again.'

'One minute,' the harsh voice counted clearly.

'I know,' said Holly, pulling the camera out of its case. 'Hold on to my waist.'

Miranda did so. 'What are you up to?' she whispered as Holly began to lean forward into the bushes, her arms outstretched.

'Taking some pictures,' said Holly.

'But we can't see a thing!'

'I know,' said Holly, leaning even further forward so that the camera was poking out of the shrubbery. 'But at least we'll get pictures of something. We'll just have to hope we're lucky.'

She pressed the shutter rapidly. *Click. Click.*

On the other side of the shrubbery feet were still pounding backwards and forwards. They could hear the sound of the van's engine, too, as if it was still running. And the cold voice again.

'One minute, thirty seconds.'

Click. Click. Click. Click. Holly took pictures as fast as she could.

'Two minutes.'

'I can't hang on much longer,' gasped Miranda.

Suddenly the van doors slammed and the voice cried, 'Go!' *Click*.

As Miranda's strength finally ran out, Holly heaved herself back out of the shrubbery. On the other side they heard the van screech away. Then everything went quiet.

Waiting until they were sure that it was clear, Holly and Miranda used the tree trunk to help them scramble back over the wall. As they dropped down to the ground, Peter was walking back towards them from the end of the lane.

'The van's gone,' he said as Holly and Miranda came up to him. 'I saw it go round the corner.'

They walked back to their bicycles. 'I wonder what they were doing?' said Miranda.

'One of them was counting time, wasn't he,' said Holly. 'As though they were timing whatever they were doing.'

'But what *were* they doing?' said Miranda. 'That's the question.'

'You mean you didn't *see*?' said Peter. 'You didn't get any pictures?'

'That's two questions,' said Miranda, as Holly handed Peter's camera back to him. 'And the answer to the first is, no, we didn't see. It was like a jungle on the other side of that wall!'

'But, yes, we did take some pictures,' said Holly. 'With luck, we'll have some that will tell us what was going on.'

'That's good,' said Peter. He flipped open his saddle-bag and carefully put the camera back on top of the metal container with his test-tubes in it. 'Mind you, it's going to be agony waiting for them to come out.'

'*If* they come out,' Holly said doubtfully.

7 Familiar faces

It was the morning after the visit to the industrial estate. With their school closed for one of its occasional days of teacher training, and the talent contest getting ever closer, Holly had suggested rehearsing their mystery sketch at her house.

By the time Miranda had arrived, though, the sun was already high in the sky and the temperature soaring.

'Do you really want to do this this morning?' Miranda had said. 'Wouldn't you prefer just to sit in a deckchair with a long, cool drink at your elbow?'

'Yes,' said Holly. 'We can rehearse tonight.'

'Phew!' gasped Miranda, plopping into the deckchair beside Holly. 'It is hot!'

'So *there* you are,' came a voice from behind them. 'I've been ringing at the doorbell for five minutes.'

Holly looked up to see Peter coming through the side gate.

'Sorry, the deckchairs are taken,' said Miranda, closing her eyes. 'You'll have to lie on the grass.'

But Peter wasn't in a mood for lying down. 'I've got the photographs,' he said, waving the packet clutched in his hand.

Holly sat up. 'That was quick.'

'I put them in at the express developers first thing this morning,' said Peter. 'I couldn't sleep last night for wondering what those men were up to.'

He undid the packet and pulled out the glossy prints. Holly and Miranda looked over his shoulders as he squatted between the deckchairs.

'Well, they came out all right,' said Miranda as she looked at the first two pictures.

'They should have done,' said Peter as they looked at the pictures of the factory and its lightning-bolt logo. 'I took them.'

'Oh, thanks very much,' said Holly.

'I didn't mean it like that,' said Peter. 'I meant that I could actually see what I was photographing, rather than poking the camera through a bush.'

Holly reached out. 'Well, let's see how I did,' she said, turning the next photograph over.

'Oh, no!'

'I thought it was only me who knew how to take awful pictures,' said Miranda.

The photograph was a perfect view of the sky.

'I hope they're not all like that,' said Peter.

'The later ones should be better,' said Holly. 'I realised I should be pointing the camera downwards.'

Peter turned over the next photograph. 'Hey – it's him! Shoe-lace!'

Caught clearly in the middle of the photograph was a tall man, with long fair hair. He seemed to be wearing an overall of some sort. Holly had only managed to capture his head and shoulders – but enough to see the shoe-lace tie at the neck of his shirt. It was the man who'd shouted at them at the car boot sale.

The next few photographs were similar. Then they turned over one with a second man in it as well – a man with a beard.

113

'Who's he?' said Miranda. 'We haven't seen him before.'

Again, Holly had captured only the top halves of both men. They seemed to be bending towards each other. In the background was the van.

'What are they doing?'

'Passing something to each other,' said Holly. 'I bet you. Something heavy.'

'A box of money?' said Peter.

'Maybe it's a big bag of coins,' said Miranda. 'Or a treasure chest. That's it, old Beardie's giving Shoe-lace a great treasure-chest full of them, all sloshing out over the sides.'

Peter grinned at her. 'We think they're printers, Miranda. You don't print coins.'

'Good thinking.' Miranda frowned. 'I was getting carried away.' She lifted herself out of the deckchair. 'Come on, isn't there a picture with their legs in it as well? That's the only way we'll find out what they're passing to each other.'

'I hope so,' said Holly. 'I was moving the camera all the time.'

They turned over picture after picture. Each was slightly different, but none were perfect. Some showed clouds, some showed ground. Most had the heads and shoulders of the two men.

And then Holly turned over the second-to-last photograph. For a moment they all stared at it, speechless. Finally Holly broke the stunned silence.

'But . . . why?'

It was the photograph they'd been waiting to see. The first that had given them a full view of the two men. They were standing at the back of the van, which had its rear doors wide open. The men's arms were outstretched, just as they had been in the previous pictures. Holly had caught them in the act of handing over . . .

'Nothing,' Holly said dumbly.

The two men had nothing in their hands.

'Maybe you took it just as they'd finished doing whatever they were doing,' said Miranda.

Peter shook his head. 'I don't think so. Look, the back of the van is empty, too.'

It was. The van's doors were wide open, clearly showing that there was nothing inside.

'Perhaps they'd been taking things out,' said Peter.

Holly examined the photograph closely.

'But if they'd finished, why do they look as though they're *still* passing things to each other?'

'It doesn't make sense,' said Miranda. 'That van raced round the back of that place as if there was no tomorrow.' She reached across to the photographs on Holly's lap. 'How about the last one?'

'It won't be any good,' said Holly, 'I was worried about falling forward. I remember I clicked the shutter just as I was trying to jump back out of those bushes. I was pointing the camera the wrong way. It won't have either of them in it.'

Miranda picked up the picture.

'Well?' asked Holly.

'You're right,' said Miranda slowly. 'It hasn't got them in it. But look who it *has* got in it!'

She handed across the photograph to Peter. It showed part of the rear of the printworks building. A window, surrounded by faded brickwork. An open door. And, standing next to it, a short, stocky man with crew-cut hair.

'The man with the money!' exclaimed Holly. 'The one who was in the driving seat of the van at the car boot sale!'

'He must have been the one doing the shouting,' said Holly. 'It sounded like it was coming from the back of the works.'

'What's he doing, though?' It was Peter, and he was peering intently at the man in the picture.

'He's got something in his hand, hasn't he?' said Holly.

The three of them studied the photograph carefully. The man seemed to be looking at something in the palm of his hand. And his thumb was sticking out.

'I've got it!' yelled Miranda. 'He's holding a stopwatch. He's timing what the other two are doing!'

Peter turned to her. 'But they're not doing anything, are they?'

Holly said, 'That doesn't make sense, Peter. They must have been doing something.'

'But what?'

'I don't know,' said Holly. She thought for a moment, then lifted herself out of her deckchair. 'But I think there's only one way of finding out. We have to go back and keep watch on that Speedi-Print place.'

Miranda groaned. 'Do we have to? It's going to be an absolute scorcher today.'

'Never mind, Miranda,' grinned Peter, pulling her to her feet. 'That's the nice thing about spying. You can do it and sunbathe at the same time.'

The real thing

In the glare of the afternoon sun, the industrial estate looked grimier than ever. As they stopped at the end of the stretch of road leading down to the waste ground and the Speedi-Print works, Holly shielded her eyes.

'How can we see what's going on round the back?' she said.

'Ride in and ask for a drink of water?' said Miranda, letting her tongue hang out.

Peter looked thoughtful. 'Perhaps we don't need to.'

'What do you mean?' said Holly.

'That driveway we saw – the one that led down to the back of the building? I bet there was a mirror mounted on the wall down there.'

'A mirror? Why should there be?'

'For safety. It helps drivers see if it's safe to go round to the back of the works.'

Holly realised what he was getting at. 'So we wouldn't have to go round the back to see what was happening? We could just look in the mirror?'

'Right.' Peter frowned. 'Although I'm not sure it helps us much. For it to work, we'd probably have to be at the end of that driveway.'

'In full view of the whole world,' said Miranda. A slow smile spread across her face. 'No problem.'

Holly looked at her. 'No disguises, Miranda. Not this time.'

'No, no, nothing like that,' called Miranda as she began to pedal down the road. 'Come on, try to keep up.'

They followed until Miranda stopped right outside the Speedi-Print building.

'That sort of mirror?' she asked, as she dismounted.

Peter stopped and glanced down the drive-way at the same time. 'Yes.'

Next to him, Holly looked too. 'And you're right, Peter. You *can* see behind the building.' In the mirror they could clearly see the back door Holly had captured in her photograph.

She looked at Miranda. 'So, how do we

stay here in the wide open without arousing suspicion?'

'Simple,' said Miranda, dismounting. 'We're helping Peter.'

'Helping me do what?'

Miranda bent down next to Peter's bike and pressed her fingernail firmly against the valve of his back tyre. 'Mend your puncture, Peter. You seem to have got a flat tyre!'

'Boring, isn't it?' said Miranda, an hour later.

'Trying to mend a puncture you haven't got,' Peter said as he pulled the inner tube from his rear tyre for the seventh time. 'I think I could do this with my eyes closed now.'

From their position on the edge of the waste ground on the opposite side of the road, Holly took another look in the mirror at the end of the driveway. At the rear of the building, all was quiet – just as it had been all the time they'd been watching.

She dipped into the saddle-bag of her own bike and pulled out the final two photographs she'd brought from their collection: the ones showing the two men passing nothing to each other, and the one of the man with the stopwatch.

'If they are forging money in there,' she said, laying the pictures on the pavement next to Miranda, 'it looks like Shoe-lace and Stopwatch are the people who are passing it on. They're the two we've seen at the car boot sales.'

'So who's this Beardie bloke?' Miranda picked up the picture with the two men in it. 'Have I seen you before, matey?' she said, turning her head this way and that as she studied the face with the beard.

'I don't think I have,' said Holly.

'No, me neither,' sighed Miranda finally. She stretched out her legs and idly picked up her pen.

Beside her Holly looked on as Peter, with much head-shaking, pretended to inspect his inner tube yet again. 'Can you pass me my puncture repair tin please, Holly?' he said loudly for the seventh time.

On the pavement, just to make the scene look real, Peter had laid out the contents of his saddle-bag. The parts of his puncture repair kit were spread out everywhere. He'd even taken out the metal tin containing his test-tubes. 'It looks like a toolbox,' he'd said when a worried Miranda had mentioned it. 'They'll think I've got serious problems.'

'If you let that stuff out, we'll *all* have serious problems!'

Holly reached across for the puncture repair tin – and saw Miranda, pen in hand.

'Miranda!'

Miranda looked startled. 'Oh, Holly. I'm sorry. I was miles away.'

At her side lay the photograph of the two men – except that, because of Miranda's doodling, the one with a beard now had a round hat on his head and an outsize pair of spectacles over his eyes.

Silently, Holly picked the photographs up and put them back in her own saddle-bag.

'I don't think I'm cut out for all this waiting around,' Miranda sighed. 'I'd prefer some action.'

'You were the one who wanted to spend the afternoon lazing in a deckchair,' retorted Holly.

'How about pumping up this tyre for me when I get my inner tube back in again?' said Peter.

'I didn't mean that sort of action,' said Miranda. 'I meant—'

She was cut short as, from the end of the road, the throaty roar of an engine reached their ears. Seconds later a van came hurtling round the corner towards them – but a different van to the one they'd expected.

'A security van?' said Holly as it bumped into the Speedi-Print driveway, raced down to the end and swung round behind the building. 'What's that here for?'

'I don't know,' said Peter. 'Delivering money? Wages, maybe?'

'Would they be getting wages if they're a fake company?' said Miranda.

'I think we're about to find out,' said Holly, her eyes glued on the mirror at the end of the driveway.

The driver of the security van leapt out. He was wearing a blue uniform and had a crash helmet on his head. Apart from his chin, the helmet's large visor covered the whole of his face. As the Mystery Kids watched he swiftly opened the rear doors of the van and took out a long oblong container.

At the same instant the rear door of the printworks was flung open.

'Shoe-lace! And Stopwatch!' gasped Miranda.

Both the men they'd seen at the car boot sale had rushed out of the door. Shoe-lace was carrying an identical container to that of the security guard who was waiting impatiently at the rear of the security van. As the Mystery Kids watched, Shoe-lace ran to the guard.

'What are they doing?' said Peter as the two men exchanged containers and Shoe-lace ran back to where Stopwatch was standing at the door with another one.

Furiously Holly dug in her saddle-bag for the photographs. In the mirror she saw Shoe-lace run out again. At the back of the van the security guard had another oblong container ready. The two men leaned towards each other as they exchanged boxes for a second time.

'That's what they're doing,' cried Holly. 'Look! Look at the photograph!'

'But they're not doing anything in the photograph,' said Miranda.

'That's just it, Miranda! They *were* doing something. They were rehearsing!'

Holly looked at the images in the mirror. More boxes were being switched over.

'That's what they've been doing all along

– rehearsing! Even down to trying out their dud notes at boot sales to see if people were fooled.'

'Rehearsing what?' said Peter.

'Swapping money boxes! Swapping boxes of good money for boxes of fakes!'

'But,' said Peter, 'that would mean the security guard is in it with them.'

'He is. He *is*! Look! It's Beardie!'

Miranda was holding the photograph and pointing at the third man. The round hat and big spectacles she'd doodled on him looked just like a security guard's helmet.

'Beardie is the security guard!' cried Miranda.

Holly looked from the picture to the man in the mirror. 'You're right, it *is* him!'

'And I *have* seen him before somewhere, I'm sure I have.' Miranda screwed her eyes up tight. 'Where, where, where . . .'

'If the security guard's in with them, that would be why they timed it all,' said Peter. 'He's probably got a fixed route. If he's not at certain places at certain times an alarm is raised. They weren't just rehearsing, Holly. They were finding out just how long they could take to swap things over without arousing suspicion.'

'But . . .' It was Holly, worried that they were missing something, '. . . what's that guard going to do with the boxes of fakes?'

'Take them back to the bank?' said Peter.

'But if he does that, they'll be spotted straight away.'

Peter nodded in agreement. 'Yes, you're right. So where *is* he taking it all?'

At the back of the printworks they'd finished loading. The security guard leapt into his driving seat and slammed his door shut.

Now, as he revved the van into life, Shoelace ran up to say something to him. The guard wound down his window and flipped up his visor at the same time.

'I know where he's taking it!' cried Miranda. 'He's taking it to the supermarket! That's where I've seen him before!'

'What?'

'Remember? Last week. Filling up the cash dispenser at the supermarket.'

'He's going there?'

'Where better?' said Peter. 'I mean, it's perfect, isn't it? Nobody would ever suspect they'd get fake money out of a cash dispenser!'

As the green van screeched out of the

driveway and roared off down the road, Holly leapt to her feet.

'Come on!' she yelled. 'We've got to go after them!'

Miranda was already yanking her bike up from the ground. 'I know a short-cut.'

'Oh, no!' It was Peter, looking forlornly at his inner tube, still hanging out from his wheel-changing exercises.

'What shall we do?'

'You go on,' yelled Peter. 'I'll catch you up as fast as I can!'

Holly and Miranda raced off down the road. Cutting corners, they pedalled on for ten minutes almost without pausing for breath.

'What if we're wrong?' Miranda yelled finally, as they were stopped in their tracks by a red traffic light. 'We don't actually *know* they were swapping good notes for dud ones, do we?'

'Miranda, what else *could* they have been doing?' Holly yelled back. 'Security vans either deliver money or they take it away, don't they? They don't deliver some *and* pick some up at the same time. What would be the point?'

'Well, I just hope we're right,'

'It won't help being right if we don't get there in time!' Holly shouted as the traffic lights switched to green. 'That security guard must be there by now. Where did you say this short-cut was?'

'Here!' shouted Miranda as they drew near to a narrow turning on their left.

Swinging round the corner, they raced along the lane. At the end, they shot between two bollards blocking the route to traffic. Round another corner they went and there, straight in front of them, was the supermarket carpark.

They'd come out on the far side of the carpark, away from the supermarket entrance itself.

'We're too late!' cried Miranda. 'Look!'

Parked outside the entrance, its windscreen shimmering in the sun, was the security van. The driving seat was empty.

'He must be inside,' said Holly, 'filling up the cash machine! Come on!'

They ran across the carpark, dodging madly between the parked cars. They raced up to the entrance.

A man was standing at the cash machine.

As Holly and Miranda dashed up, they saw the 'UNABLE TO DISPENSE CASH' message flick off. The man, who had been about to leave, turned back and slipped his cash card into the machine.

'He must have just finished filling it up,' said Miranda. 'He'll be out any minute.'

The man at the cash dispenser began to key in the amount he wanted.

Holly looked around desperately. How could they stop the guard getting away? They had to prove he'd filled the machine with fake money. But how?

Suddenly, as she saw a woman hurrying out of the supermarket, Holly saw how. It was the supermarket's manageress.

'Excuse me! Please!' Holly raced over to the manageress. 'I was with my friend Peter last week. He had a forged ten-pound note. Remember?'

'Of course I do,' smiled the manageress.

'I haven't got time to explain,' gasped Holly. 'But . . .'

She pointed over to the cash dispenser as it whirred and started to rattle out money. 'That machine. It's just been filled with fake notes!'

'What?'

'Holly! The guard! He's coming out!'

Miranda was pointing. Through the plate glass windows, the security guard was hurrying out from the inner office, followed by an assistant manager holding a set of keys.

Holly turned to the manageress. 'You've got to believe us. Please!'

As the man at the cash machine collected his money, Holly leapt in front of him. 'Excuse me,' said Holly, 'can this lady please check those notes?'

'I beg your pardon?'

'I think they're forgeries,' said Holly. 'Please!'

The man looked very uncertain. Then, seeing the badge on the manageress's lapel, he handed over the bank-notes he'd just taken from the cash dispenser.

The manageress looked very seriously at Holly as she took the notes. 'If this is some kind of joke . . .' she began.

'It isn't!' pleaded Holly. The security guard had almost reached the swishing glass doors. 'Quick. Before he gets away!'

'He won't!' yelled Miranda.

A long snake of shopping trolleys was

standing beside the entrance. Seizing hold of the end trolley, Miranda pushed with all her might.

'Mind your backs! Excuse me! Mind your backs!'

Moments later, the snake of trolleys was totally blocking the doorway. Nobody could get in or out.

'Get these things out of my way!' growled the security guard as he found his way barred.

'Sorry,' said Miranda, pushing the trolleys even more firmly into position. 'Learner driver. I just can't seem to get the hang of these at all.'

Next to Holly, the manageress was holding the first of the man's bank-notes up to the light.

'Well?' said Holly, her heart pounding like a drum.

The manageress looked at her – then shook her head. 'It's fine. Nothing wrong with it at all.'

'What!'

'It's what I said. A perfectly good five-pound note.'

Over in the doorway, the security guard

had finally forced Miranda's snake of trolleys out of the way and shoved his way past them.

'What about the other ones?' she said desperately.

With a sigh, the manageress lifted another note and inspected it. 'Perfect. A perfectly good five-pound note.'

Holly's mind whirled. Why? All the clues fitted together. They *had* to be forging ten-pound notes.

Ten-pound notes! Not five-pound notes. In her mind's eye, Holly saw the back of the cash machine as they'd seen it through the open door. The four hoppers for notes. He'd only replaced the ten-pound note hoppers!

'What about the ten-pound notes?' cried Holly, pointing to the rest of the man's money. 'What about them?'

Reluctantly, the manageress held one of the man's ten-pound notes up to the bright sunlight.

A look of surprise crossed her face. She looked at Holly – then at the security guard, now glancing over his shoulder at them as he hurried back to his van.

'It's a forgery,' she said.

She held another of the man's ten-pound notes up to the light, then another. 'This one is, too! And this.'

Holly swung round.

'Stop him, somebody!'

But the guard was already on the move, sprinting hard. All around people were standing and staring, but none moved to stop him.

Leaping into his van, the guard slammed the door shut. Through the open window, Holly and Miranda saw him struggling to start the engine.

'Peter!' screamed Miranda. 'Watch out!'

While they'd been concentrating on what the guard was doing, the two girls hadn't noticed Peter racing into the carpark on his bike – right in front of the van!

Suddenly the van's engine roared into life as the security guard finally managed to start it. Reversing back to give himself room to avoid Peter's bike as it lay on the ground in front of him, the guard screeched his van away from the kerb.

'Get out of the way!' screamed Holly.

With the van roaring towards him, Peter had stepped out in front of it.

The guard blasted on the van's horn. Still Peter didn't move . . . until, with the van only metres away, he suddenly leapt to one side.

'What's he doing?'

'He's got something in his hand!' yelled Miranda.

What, they couldn't see. But, whatever it was, as the van roared past him, Peter tossed it hard through the driver's open window.

'Peter! Are you all right?' said Holly, dashing up to him. 'I thought you were going to be knocked down.'

'So did I,' said Miranda. 'Don't you ever do anything like that again.'

She looked out towards the carpark exit. People were chasing after the security van now, but it was too late. The guard had almost made his escape.

'You could have been killed,' Miranda said. 'And for nothing. He's getting away anyhow.'

'I wouldn't be so sure about that,' grinned Peter. He pointed out towards the carpark exit, as the security van slowed – and stopped!

'He's getting out!'

As they watched, the driver's door was

135

flung open. Half-jumping, half-falling, the security guard left his van, only to be immediately overpowered by chasing shoppers!

Holly and Miranda looked at Peter in amazement.

'Peter Hamilton, what on earth did you throw into that van?'

'A test-tube?' laughed Holly. 'Of your stink solution? No wonder he stopped.'

'It was the only thing I could think of,' said Peter. 'I thought of it as I was putting everything back into my saddle-bag outside the printworks. I remembered him opening his window to talk to Shoe-lace and thought that if I got to the supermarket in time, he'd still be inside. I was going to tip it over his seat.'

'But he was already driving off when you arrived.'

'So all I could do was to toss one of the test-tubes through his window.' He laughed. 'After taking the cork out, of course.'

'No wonder he stopped!' said Holly.

She looked at the supermarket manageress, and the policeman sitting beside her. Both were looking slightly mystified.

'Peter's stink solution is *very* powerful,' she explained.

'But I thought that stuff only worked when it got hot,' said Miranda.

Peter pointed out of the office window at the sun, only now starting to sink lower in the clear blue sky.

'After being in the sun all afternoon while we pretended to be changing my tyre?' he said. 'Miranda, that solution was boiling!'

Everybody laughed.

'So, mystery solved,' said the police officer. 'And we were just in time to catch the other pair.'

'Shoe-lace and Stopwatch?' said Holly.

'If that's who they were,' said the policeman. 'They were caught red-handed with the good money the security guard had given them. And, when we searched the place, we found the whole set-up was fake.'

'Just like the money they'd been making.'

'That's right. They didn't do any real printing at all. It was just a front for their forgery operation. And a big one at that.'

'Really?' said Peter.

'Oh, yes. That security guard had a whole list of cash machines he was due to go to.'

'Oh, yes, not just us,' said the supermarket manageress. She smiled broadly. 'There are an awful lot of shops and banks in the area who have got you three to thank.'

'They have?' said Miranda, her eyes lighting up. 'How?'

'Miranda!' cried Holly.

The policeman grinned. 'Miranda is right,' he said. 'You do deserve a reward.'

'There you are,' said Miranda. 'Did you have anything special in mind?'

'As it happens, I did,' said the policeman, looking out through the office window which overlooked the supermarket floor. He dug into his trousers pocket for some money. 'The doughnuts are on me.'

'No, no.' It was the manageress. 'I'm sorry. I can't allow that.'

'Why ever not?'

The manageress smiled broadly. 'Because the doughnuts are on *me*.'

'Oh, let's not argue about it,' said Holly. She linked arms with Peter and Miranda. 'The doughnuts can be on both of you!'

THE MYSTERY KIDS SERIES
FIONA KELLY

61989 9	SPY-CATCHERS!	£2.99	☐
61990 2	LOST AND FOUND	£2.99	☐
61991 0	TREASURE HUNT	£2.99	☐
61992 9	THE EMPTY HOUSE	£2.99	☐
61993 7	SMUGGLERS BAY	£2.99	☐
61994 5	FUNNY MONEY	£2.99	☐
65356 6	BLACKMAIL!	£2.99	☐
65565 8	MYSTERY WEEKEND	£2.99	☐
65566 6	WRONG NUMBER	£2.99	☐
65567 4	HOSTAGE	£2.99	☐
65568 2	BOX OF TRICKS	£2.99	☐
65569 0	KIDNAP!	£2.99	☐

All Hodder Children's books are available at your local bookshop or newsagent, or can be ordered direct from the publisher. Just tick the titles you want and fill in the form below. Prices and availability subject to change without notice.

Hodder Children's Books, Cash Sales Department, Bookpoint, 39 Milton Park, Abingdon, OXON, OX14 4TD, UK. If you have a credit card you may order by telephone – 01235 831700.

Please enclose a cheque or postal order may payable to Bookpoint Ltd to the value of the cover price and allow the following for postage and packing: UK & BFPO:- £1.00 for the first book, 50p for the second book, and 30p for each additional book ordered up to a maximum charge of £3.00.
OVERSEAS & EIRE:- £2.00 for the first book, £1.00 for the second book, and 50p for each additional book.

Name ....

Address ....

....

....

If you would prefer to pay by credit card, please complete:
Please debit my Visa/Access/Diner's Card/American Express (delete as applicable) card no:

Signature ....

Expiry Date ....